So Long at the Fair

Also by Hadley Irwin

Kim/Kimi
Abby, My Love
Bring to a Boil and Separate
Moon and Me
What About Grandma?
I Be Somebody
(MARGARET K. MCELDERRY BOOKS)

The Lilith Summer
We Are Mesquakie, We Are One

So Long at the Fair

Hadley Irwin

Margaret K. McElderry Books

NEW YORK

Margaret K. McElderry Books
Macmillan Publishing Company
866 Third Avenue
New York, NY 10022
Collier Macmillan Canada, Inc.

First Edition
Printed in the United States of America
10 9 8 7 6 5 4 3 2 1

Composition by PennSet Inc.
Bloomsburg, Pennsylvania
Printed and bound by R. R. Donnelley & Sons
Harrisonburg, Virginia
Designed by Barbara A. Fitzsimmons

Library of Congress Cataloging-in-Publication Data

Irwin, Hadley.
So long at the fair.
Summary: The summer fairgrounds provide a temporary refuge for eighteen-year-
old Joel as he struggles to deal with his memories of Ashley, the friend he loved
and expected to have as a part of his life always.
[1. Fairs—Fiction. 2. Friendship—Fiction.
3. Death—Fiction] I. Title.
PZ7.I712So 1988   [Fic]   88–12813
ISBN 0–689–50454–3

For all of you who wait for tomorrow

PART I

Joel Wendell Logan III

I was about to slither into my freshman year of college. Ashley had left without telling me why. My parents were off for a week at the lake. The time was not only ripe, it was rotten—or rotting—I wasn't sure which. It didn't really matter. Ashley would have said, "Who cares?"

There was Ashley again, just when I didn't want to remember, but she had always been in my life: one step ahead of me, one point above me in every test, one second quicker to see the fallacy in some teacher's logic. Let's face it. Ashley was the genius of the TAGS. That's what we were: Talented and Gifted, the whole bunch of us, ever since grade school.

What a joke! Talented if it meant we were smarter than most of our teachers. Gifted, in my case, if it meant living on the north side with a trust fund from a grandfather and having a doctor father who'd made it big on his own. Gifted, with a house too big for three people who were seldom there at the same time, a Porsche in the garage, a pool that could have been used for Olympic events.

Once, when I was a little kid, Aunt Elise gave me a kaleidoscope, not the cardboard kind that you can find in any kids' store, but a solid brass one that came from one of those catalogues that advertise stuff for the executive who has everything. I'm sure it cost a lot, not that it mattered, but my parents thought it was right up there with genuine primitive folk art, which was very big back then. I was young, six or seven, and I spent hours looking through the thing, turning it to make patterns that kept changing. Because it seemed like magic or because I was always supposed to put it up on the shelf in the library when I was finished, it was a source of fascination and mystery. Besides, I knew it was full of fragments of semiprecious stones; at least that's what my parents told me.

Mostly because I was curious and partly because semiprecious sounded like the polished stones the gardener used around our flower beds, I broke the thing apart in order to discover the magic. It took a long time with a hammer and screwdriver and chisel, and all I ended up with were broken mirrors and colored stones. Mother sighed. Father shook his head, and the maid cleaned up the mess.

I stopped believing in magic.

I forgot all about that toy until last summer, the

summer after my *world* splintered, cracked open, and fell apart. I suppose it was a time with its own kind of magic, though I didn't recognize it then. When I remember that summer, I never think "*I* did that." It's more "*Joe* did that"—a Joe who was me once, but not the Joel I'm becoming.

PART II

Joe Logan

The lights of the State Fair's midway spilled across the hill like a handful of colored glass. Even from where Joe stood, he could hear the shrieks and squeals from the amusement rides, the harsh cries of barkers, the crazy mixture of music booming from amplifiers in front of the girlie shows, and behind it all, the stock cars roaring around the race track.

He was dressed right: faded jeans, a shirt that should have been thrown away years ago, a sweater that was fraying at the cuffs. No, the sweater was wrong. He'd knotted the sleeves around his neck, which would have been fine at the club if he'd just come off the tennis courts, but here was different. He didn't want to be somebody. He wanted to be anybody, just one more eighteen-year-old kid come to the city to take in the fair. He pulled off the sweater and retied the sleeves around his waist so that the tail hung down to the backs of his knees. Much better.

The closer he got to the entry gates, the more the sounds enveloped him like a stereo he couldn't turn down. Was it possible to blast out thoughts by sheer noise? It hadn't worked at home the last few days after Mom and Dad left for the lake. He'd turned on every TV and radio in the whole house, but he still could see it all as if a never-ending tape had been inserted in his brain.

Once inside the fairgrounds he gave up trying to forget and let the crowd swirl around him until he was carried past the grandstand and into the heart of the midway itself.

"Step right up."

"Try your luck."

"Guess your weight."

"Read your palm."

"Step out of this world."

Sure. Step out of this world! He'd like to, but whose world could he step into? There were as many worlds as there were people, each wrapped up in little plastic bubbles of self. A person was lucky if he could understand his own world, let alone anyone else's.

Joe strolled along, looking into the blank faces of strangers. A merry-go-round wheezed to a stop, but Joe's head kept on throbbing to the flat beat of the mechanical music. He leaned against the counter of a food stand and watched a kid—he couldn't have been more than thirteen—spear a hot dog on a stick, dip it into a yellow mass of cornmeal and plunge it into a pot of boiling grease. The smell should have been sickening, but it wasn't and the corn dog that he bought from the kid tasted even better than it smelled. The only trouble was the corn dog kept on tasting, grease coating his teeth and tongue like cold lard. The cholesterol count of what he had eaten would have taken care of his family for a year, and his father, the doctor, and his mother, the calorie counter, would have had him on a stomach pump at the last swallow. Both Mom and Dad were probably sitting in a lakeside restaurant now, confronted by a leaf of something green touched by a soupçon of raspberry vinaigrette.

He moved on, trying to look inconspicuous. Ashley told him once, "Joel, you're too sway-vee to get lost in a crowd."

"It's swahv, not sway-vee," he'd corrected her.

"I know, but I like sway-vee better. It has less class."

Ashley never had to worry about class. She was class.

He stopped again to watch a woman weave a mist of cotton candy around a cardboard cone, piling the sugared threads into a bouffant pink magic. He bought one, took a huge bite, and felt it melt, gritty and sweet, over the grease of the corn dog.

One bite was enough. It was like chewing on Christmas tree angel hair. He looked around for a trash can, but before he could move, the cardboard cone was pulled from his hand and he was facing a crowd of people, pointing at him and laughing.

A monkey in cap and vest, holding Joe's cotton candy, jumped up on an old man's shoulder and chattered away as if acknowledging the applause and laughter. Before Joe could move on, a mime—boy or girl, man or woman, he couldn't tell which—face painted white and dressed in blouse and pantaloons, knelt before him with clasped hands as if apologizing for the antics of the monkey. With exaggeration, the mime wiped away make-believe tears, leaped to its feet, and in one whirling motion retrieved the cotton candy cone and with a sweeping bow offered it to him as if it were a king's treasure.

The crowd roared. Joe, half embarrassed, laughed too. He wasn't used to being laughed at; in fact, he wasn't used to laughing these last few months.

Quickly, before people moved away, the monkey did a backward somersault, came up holding a tin cup, and darted into the crowd. Dimes and quarters jingled into the cup, but when he came to Joe, he set the cup on the ground and went through the same gestures as the mime had. Joe reached for the loose change in his pocket, and then with a shrug pulled out a twenty-dollar bill and dropped it into the cup. His father would not have approved, nor his mother. They'd spent half his life teaching him percentages for tips: so much for a dinner tab, this much to a cab driver, that much to a hotel maid, and he'd just paid twenty dollars for a recycled cotton candy cone. Why not?

Balancing his cotton candy in one hand, he strolled on, trying to look nonchalant. Ashley used to tease him by saying he walked like a politician, drumming up votes. He had never bothered to figure out whether Ashley really meant what she said or if she just enjoyed hearing herself say it.

"Hey, kid!" It was the monkey man, holding out the twenty-dollar bill. "Did ya make a mistake back there? We're good, but do you think you can afford this?"

He had made a dumb mistake. If he was pretending to be a kid on a once-a-year trip to the State Fair, he wouldn't drop twenty bucks like that. Joe reached in his pocket, pulled out a wrinkled one-dollar bill and held it out in exchange. "Gee. Thanks a lot. This was supposed to last me all week."

The monkey man stuffed the bill in his pocket. "You must be crazy, kid, if you think you can hang around here for a week on twenty bucks. Unless you're camping here with your folks. You exhibiting stock or something?"

"Yeah. Right. My parents and I . . . I mean me and my folks are staying up there." He waved his hand toward the darkness beyond the midway, hoping he'd pointed in the right direction. It was hard to pretend to need when you didn't need anything. Ashley was right. They'd both had too much—too much of everything. But if the man thought Joe was a farm kid, maybe that's what he would be.

He wandered off toward the barns, walking through narrow hay-dusty aisles between pens of grunting, mooing, bleating, bellowing beasts. He viewed enough sheep to cure the most incurable insomniac, enough pigs to supply a packing plant, and enough chickens and turkeys to take care of decades of holiday dinners. He may not have looked like a stock exhibitor when he had completed his tour, but he knew he smelled like one.

A whole night to kill. A night? Weeks of nights! A month of them, really, before he started in at the university, and time loomed ahead like one big yawn. He walked through displays of farm machinery, new cars, household appliances. He watched a tractor pull, a tug-of-war in mud, a water fight between some small towns' firemen, and sat through a performance of a rock band.

An August chill settled over the grounds and he pulled on his sweater. He should head for home. It was a silly idea, thinking that he could lose himself at a fair—that coming back would help make some sense out of what had happened. He had once read of an experiment where people who were told *not* to think about polar bears found themselves thinking about polar bears all the time. Ashley was *his* polar bear.

An old-time fiddler was sawing out a square-dance tune from a makeshift stage set up in the middle of a park. Joe found a bench and sat down, not to listen, but to watch people stream by. What was it about the faces of strangers that looked so indifferent? And beards—how many kinds could men concoct: tiny upper-lip fringes, sweeping moustaches, goatees, full beards drooping down from the ears and covering half the face with just enough space left for a mouth. And women and their earrings: dangling hoops, crescents, triangles, medallions, dots, splinters, bars. And hairdos: cropped and sleek as if the hair were molded onto the skull, mats of bushy curls, masses of wavy fluff, shoulder-length cascades, braids, windblown puffs.

He was switching to men's hats when the fiddler

fiddled to a stop and bowed out to spotty applause, to be replaced by a skinny girl with a guitar who hoisted herself up onto a stool in front of the microphone, adjusted the guitar strap around her shoulders, and began to sing in a pure, soft voice that cut through the distant shouts of barkers and loudspeakers trying to locate lost children:

> *Oh dear, what can the matter be?*
> *Oh dear, what can the matter be?*
> *Oh dear, what can the matter be?*
> *Johnny's so long at the fair.*

Joe ceased his people-watching and leaned forward. He hadn't been listening when the emcee in cowboy hat and jeans had announced the girl.

> *He promised to bring me a pretty blue ribbon.*
> *He promised to bring me a pretty blue ribbon.*

The voice was like a thread of silver in the night air, with never a waver, but clear and natural as a cardinal's call.

> *He promised to bring me a pretty blue ribbon*
> *To tie up my bonnie brown hair.*

People strolling by stopped to listen. Then, without waiting for applause and with a strum or two of chords, she slipped into a folk song that Joe had learned years ago in grade school. He sat entranced as she sang tune after tune without pause, and then, with a half curtsey, left the platform.

Joe stayed on through a harmonica player, a one-man band, a baton twirler, and finally a kitchen band of kazoos. He stood up ready to leave when a voice said, "Did you give up on cotton candy?"

He whirled around, and there was the girl who belonged to the "bonnie brown hair" song, only the hair was not "bonnie brown." It was mousey blond framing a too-thin face and eyes that looked as if they should belong to someone else.

"Beg pardon?" he said; then, remembering the farm kid he was trying to be, added, "Run that by me again."

"I asked you if you'd given up on cotton candy."

"Oh, you mean . . ." Joe tugged at his sweater. "You saw all that? My getting ripped off by a monkey?"

"Sure I saw it. I work with the monkey. I'm the mime."

"You're what?"

"The mime. A girl's got to eat, and I've grown fond of eating and the job pays."

"But you sing."

"For free. Here." She pointed to the stage. "But Henry pays me to be a mime. And as I said, I like food. Speaking of eating, want to come have a cup of coffee with me? I'll buy."

"Well . . . I . . . I don't believe so," Joe stuttered. "You see . . . I'm . . ."

"Don't be alarmed. I'm not trying to con you." She looked as innocent as the girl next door.

"Do you always pick up strangers and offer to buy coffee?"

"Never!" Her eyes crinkled into slits when she smiled. "But my horoscope for today said I'd meet a tall, handsome stranger. I'm Aries and my moon is in its ascendency, you see."

He didn't see, but she took his arm and was steering him back toward the midway.

"You work here on the grounds?" she asked.

"Sort of," he said. "I mean I want to. I'm looking for a job." He glanced down at her. She was too plain to be pretty, but too different to be plain. His mother would have missed a putt if she ever thought her son would pick up a girl like this at a fair. Of course, he hadn't. She'd picked him up, and he wondered how long it would take her to see if he still had his twenty-dollar bill. It was turning into a game.

"Red serves the biggest cup of coffee on the grounds," she said, pointing to a makeshift booth with counters and benches still smelling like fresh-cut lumber. "Best hamburgers too."

She ordered the hamburger. He ordered just coffee although he hadn't eaten since the cotton candy. He wanted to order a burger, but he'd wait to see if she was really going to pay or stick him not only for his coffee but for her hamburger too. He tried not to look when she dipped into the catsup and he could almost taste the pickle and onion as she bit into the oversized bun. He couldn't remember ever being as hungry as he was right then, but he sipped on the black coffee as if he were enjoying it.

"You live around here?" she asked, her mouth full of hamburger.

"Naw. Just passing through. Thought maybe I could pick up a job."

"How long you been on the road?"

"Week or so."

It *was* fun. It was like being in a play, and he really had become the person he was pretending to be.

"Where you heading?"

"Colorado. Ski resort. I know a guy out there."

"You don't look like a ski bum to me."

"How come?"

"You don't smell as if you'd been on the road."

"I had a shower this morning." He sipped his

coffee. She took another bite from her hamburger.

"That monkey man your grandfather?"

She almost choked. "Old Henry? No! I started working for him after I got out of high school. I've been following him around to all the fairs this summer, seeing if I can get enough money ahead to cut a good tape and send it down to Nashville. I'm going to make it some day in country western."

Joe, caught with a mouthful of coffee, sputtered, "Really?"

"Sure." She sopped up the catsup from the paper plate with the last bit of bun. "A fortune-teller told me that once, that I'd make it big."

He wanted to tell her the world was full of guitar-strumming idiots thinking they were going to make it big, but instead he doodled a circle in the wet ring his coffee cup had left on the counter.

"Say, that's lucky!"

"What's lucky?"

"What you're doing. Making circles in your coffee."

"Don't tell me you're superstitious."

"No. I just believe. But I suppose whatever I believe, and other people don't, can be called superstition."

He wiped his hand against his trouser leg. "Well, anyway, I think you've certainly got the voice to make it."

"I know." She picked up the last crumb with her forefinger.

"Just one problem. Life's never fair. It's not what you know. It's who you know." He was sounding like his father.

"Who says? But I'm going to keep trying. That's part of living, the trying." She looked up and grinned. "Life is trying. How's that for a motto. It can have a double meaning, can't it? Think about it."

He thought about it briefly. Neither he nor Ashley had ever really tried for anything that he could remember. If he wanted something he got it. He didn't have to try for it.

"Say, look . . ." he began. "My name's Joe. What's yours? I mean what should I call you?"

"You don't really have to call me anything. Are you going to stick around here at the fair?"

"Why not?" he said. It was an Ashley answer. "If I can find a job."

She reached into her pocket and pulled out a dollar bill and a handful of change. She *was* paying, and he let her.

"Thanks a lot for the coffee."

"That's okay. If you get a job and stick around, you can buy next time. Now I need some sleep."

"I'll walk with you. Where you going?"

"Back to the camper. It's Henry's. He and Mic—

that's the monkey—sleep out in a tent. I get the camper. Where are you staying?"

"Oh, with a couple of guys. Over in the barns." He didn't worry about the lie. After all, the girl didn't matter.

The crowds were emptying from the midway as he left the dismal camper. She had never told him her name, but what difference did it make? He wondered if he could still catch a taxi home. He didn't feel like walking through the South Flats alone at midnight. But why go home? No one was there. What would a farm kid do, alone at the State Fair if all he had in his pocket was twenty dollars . . . no job and no place to sleep?

So for lack of anything better to do, Joe stayed on at the fair.

It wasn't the sounds or the smell of the cow barns that woke him the next morning. It was hunger. He stretched. Bales of hay were no water bed, but they were free. He shook the dried alfalfa leaves from his hair and brushed off his sweater and trousers and headed for the nearest smell of coffee, coming from a food tent already packed with exhibitors from the various barns.

He loaded his tray with pancakes, bacon, scrambled eggs, toast, milk, and coffee and reached into his pocket to pay the lady sitting at a card table.

"That'll be four dollars and fifty-seven cents, please," the lady said, rearranging her bills and change in a muffin tin.

He searched through all his pockets. His twenty-dollar bill was gone! He had left his billfold and credit cards along with his checkbook on the dresser at home. He stood looking at the woman, holding out two one-dollar bills and a single quarter. "I'm sorry. This is all I can find. I had a twenty last night but . . ." His voice trailed off and he felt what he knew must be a blush, even though he'd seldom had occasion to blush before in his life. He knew the humiliation that was coming. He'd been with his parents in a New York restaurant when a man had ordered a splashy dinner for friends and then tried to duck out from the bill.

"Would you like me to take something back?" he asked, aware of the line of people waiting behind him.

"Young man, you owe the Friends Church of Bear Creek two dollars and thirty-two cents. If you don't eat that breakfast here, it will be cold and worth not even that much. You may return and pay us later today, or, if you'd care to contribute your time, you could spend an hour clearing tables and emptying garbage for us. We're short on help this morning. Why don't you eat and make up your mind so that the people behind you can sit down?" She took his money and motioned toward a table.

Food had never tasted so good. The pancakes—buttermilk—melted in his mouth without his even chewing and the maple syrup was, he was sure, straight from a sugar maple tree and the eggs and milk country fresh, with home-cured bacon. But the twenty-dollar bill. He remembered taking it from the monkey man and slipping it into his hip pocket. Someone had ripped him off while he slept, or, more likely, the nameless girl with her cup of coffee . . . Sure. It was that simple. She'd picked his pocket, and he thought he'd been playing a game with her. She'd probably been the one who taught the monkey to steal.

He could feel the lady at the money table watching him as he ate, not an out-and-out stare, but a quick little twitch of her black eyes in his direction. Did he look like some slick kid who would try to sneak out? He downed the last of his milk, stacked his dishes on the tray, drew in a big breath, and approached the money table.

"You ready, son?" The woman smiled, her face falling into a series of dimpled wrinkles. She was wearing a hair net that made it appear as if she had on a cap of gray, and although she was sitting, there was no visible evidence of a stool or chair beneath her generous proportions.

"I'm ready," Joe answered.

"Wanda!" the woman shouted over her shoulder. "Come get this boy and put him to work. He's volunteered to help us."

A tiny Wanda emerged from behind a steaming pancake grill, wiping her face with the corner of her apron. "Let's see your hands, son," she said, her head cocked to one side, looking like an inquisitive sparrow.

Obediently he held out his hands, wondering why he hadn't just promised to show up later with the money. He was sure they would have believed a promise. Besides, what was the big deal about a couple of dollar bills and some loose change?

"Dishwasher," Wanda announced. "Doesn't have enough calluses for garbage. Earl and Clyde can take care of the garbage when they get here." She turned toward the kitchen. "Come on. What's your name, anyway?"

"Joe," he said. "Where's the dishwasher and what do I put in it?"

Wanda laughed, a big laugh from such a small woman. She was still laughing as she called out to the other women who were busy at the stove.

"Maude, Leah, Velma . . . this is Joe. He's here to help out. Wants to know where the dishwasher is." She brushed tears from her eyes.

The women looked up from their work and the laughing began again. "You," one of them said, "you're the dishwasher. There's the tub. Here's the dishes, and we're running short on coffee cups so wash them first."

In their aprons and printed housedresses, sturdy, no-nonsense shoes, they looked as if they had spent their lives in a kitchen doing just what they were doing now. They were all about the same age as his grandmother, who was probably playing tennis down in Florida, but they looked much older, like old apples that had tree-ripened too long. Still, there was a calmness about them as if they had accepted their age as a natural result of having lived.

Joe, elbow deep in hot suds, attacked the pile of bulky coffee cups, scrubbing with a frayed dishcloth, as Wanda had directed, "around the rim four or five times and dip them three times in scalding water." Of course, he'd known people did wash dishes by hand, but the extent of his experience was putting stuff in the dishwasher on the maid's day off. He was making satisfactory progress on the pile of cups when he reached for another stack with his soapy hands only to have the top two cups teeter and tip and crash against the galvanized washtub.

The cups skittered across the floor, with two handles taking off in opposite directions.

"Whoops!" he shouted, but the women went on about their work as if nothing had happened. "I'll . . . I'll pay you," he said, squatting down to retrieve the pieces. "I mean I'll keep working."

Wanda swished by, balancing another plate of freshly made pancakes. "Never mind. If it's supposed to happen, it will."

He plunged his hands into the suds and continued to scrub and dip. Actually it wasn't so bad after he had set the last cup in the draining rack. There was something sort of soothing in the repetition; even his anger at the girl and his lost twenty-dollar bill faded as he listened to the women talking and was caught up in the rhythm of wash, rinse, wash, rinse.

One of the women—the tall sturdy one—Maude, he thought, or maybe Velma—picked up the heavy trayful of coffee mugs as if it were a pan of feathers and headed for the dining area. "You did good with the cups," she muttered.

"That pile of silverware's next," Wanda ordered as she hurried by with a plate of still-sizzling bacon.

Joe decided the poet who complained his life was measured out with coffee spoons wasn't lying, for Wanda kept stopping by and inspecting the spoons he'd already washed. Forks were next and he almost flunked them. She tossed two or three back at him.

"Don't just swish them around. Wash them! You wash *between* the tines." He got knives down to a science: a swish down and a swish up and a toss into the scalding water.

"Watch out for the pans. They're greasy and you'll need more hot water."

He'd thought he was through.

"The scouring pads are over there."

After the first greasy pan, he would have gladly washed an entire restaurantful of coffee mugs. Not only did the pans have to be scoured, they had to pass Wanda's inspection, and Wanda, he was learning, was no pushover when it came to pans.

"Well," she finally announced, "that should just about do it until lunch. Here, wipe your hands. Elsie wants to see you up at the cashier table."

His skin was puckered clear up to his elbows and his hair was as wet from sweat as if he had stood in a shower. And what he wouldn't give for a shower.

"Well, young man," Elsie said, riffling through the bills in her muffin pan. "You earned your pancakes. Now if you will help Elmer and Clyde empty the garbage pails"—she held out two dollar bills—"you will have earned all that you owe and more."

He would have gladly gone back to his dishwashing tub after a trip on the garbage detail with Clyde. One glance into the garbage can before

Clyde pressed the lid down was enough to cause Joe to wish he had not eaten breakfast.

"Why don't you use garbage bags?" Joe asked as he lugged his side of the thirty-gallon can over to a pickup truck with a rusting stock tank in the back.

"This is for the pigs. Waste not . . ."

"Want not," Joe muttered with a final heave on the garbage pail. "You mean you feed this stuff to your pigs?"

"Makes the tenderest ham you've ever tasted."

Joe considered never tasting ham again. After the last garbage can he was certain.

"Now," Clyde said, leaning up against the truck, "if you'll take them three cans over there to that hose and clean them out, we'll be done. I got a slipped disc and that bending over that way really gets to me."

Joe hosed out the cans.

"Well, that should just about do it," Clyde finally said peering into the cans. "If you get hungry, come back at lunch. The womenfolks could use you."

Joe drew in a deep breath as he left the church stand. He was sure he would never be hungry again. Did everyone have to work that hard for a breakfast and two dollars and thirty-two cents? It couldn't be. His clothes smelled of stale pancakes. His hair was full of grease. He'd chuck it all and head home to the pool and the sauna and the air-conditioning.

He'd get a taxi and pay for it with the money he'd left on his dresser. But first he'd spend the money he'd earned scrubbing pans for the old ladies. It took two seconds to decide how to spend it.

The plastic toothbrush cost sixty-five cents and a tube of toothpaste took most of the rest. He was just turning away from the counter to look for a washroom when he heard her voice.

"You're beginning to look real. At least you smell real, or maybe I mean you really smell." It was that girl again, hands on her hips, looking like an escapee from junior high.

"What do you mean real?" If what Joe felt was real, he'd settle for illusion any time. Then remembering his missing twenty, he added, "Have you spent it already? Or did I just subsidize your demo record?"

"What are you talking about?"

"My twenty bucks!"

"Henry said he gave it back to you. He did, didn't he?"

"Sure. And he saw where I put it too, didn't he? In my hip pocket."

"What are you saying? That Henry . . ."

"All I'm saying is that I was ripped off, and you're the only person I talked to last night."

She started to walk away, then turned, her face flushed. "I am a singer. I am a mime. I am *not* a pickpocket. And any dunce would know you don't walk around a fairgrounds with a twenty-dollar bill in your hip pocket where any smart aleck kid can lift it."

"But . . ." he began and then couldn't figure out how to finish the sentence.

The girl walked back toward him and stopped a mere foot away. "Look, buddy. Anyone on the road knows that you don't go to sleep with money in your pocket. You stuff it in your boots and you keep your boots on. So you can just take your 'but' and stuff *that*!"

He couldn't think of an answer and she didn't wait for one. He stood holding his toothbrush and toothpaste as she disappeared in the morning crowd.

Clean teeth should have made him feel better, but they didn't. He should have found a cab and gone home, but he hadn't. He should have apologized to the crazy girl—have said, "I'm sorry." He tried to remember the last time he had told anyone he was sorry, but all he could think of was that cold fall day when he had looked up through pine trees and whispered, "I'm sorry, Ashley." But that had been too late to change anything.

It was an empty feeling in his stomach that he wasn't too sure was really hunger that took him back to Elsie and her church food stand.

"Could you use an experienced dishwasher for the rest of the day?"

Elsie gave him an up-and-down inspection, moving only her eyes, and shouted, "Wanda!"

Wanda's head appeared like magic again from behind a shelf of home-baked pies. "What is it, Elsie?"

"Could we use our dishwasher again?"

Elsie's "our" was more gratifying by far than Bradgate High's Most-Likely- to-Succeed-Award he'd won last spring at the graduation he didn't attend.

"Send him back," Wanda called, and pulling off his sweater, Joe went back to the tub, rolled up his sleeves, and plunged his hands into the hot suds. He worked the lunch shift, the afternoon garbage haul, the dinner shift, and even the mop-up detail. When he finally checked out with Elsie, his arms from his elbows down were like two withered stumps and his back felt as if someone had been pounding on his spine.

"You've eight dollars coming, over and beyond your board, son." If it had been eight hundred dollars, he couldn't have felt better.

"Could I have three dollars now, and you keep the rest for me till I come back tomorrow?"

"Certainly," Elsie said with a decisive nod. "How many tomorrows do you have?" She had eyes that could immobilize, like Miss Wright's in junior-high math.

"I don't know."

"You should think on that, my boy. Life is not something to be squandered." She counted out three dollar bills. "*Nor* is money."

"Oh, I won't squander it," Joe promised with so much sincerity he almost believed himself.

He hurried through the crowd over to the park. A troupe of local tap dancers were clattering around the stage about half a beat behind the recorded music booming through the loudspeakers. They were truly awful, but the crowd applauded and shouted approval until they launched into a ragged encore. When they finally jounced off the stage for the last time the emcee returned. "Friends and neighbors, welcome to our last act of the evening. Let's give a great big hand to a little girl with a great big voice and here she is. Our own Kentucky Rose."

People left, relatives of the tap dancers, Joe guessed, and more people took their places—older couples laden with paper shopping bags bulging with giveaways, teenagers in Levis and T-shirts with school names printed on them, exhausted-looking young couples carrying babies or pushing strollers with balloons tied to them.

Kentucky Rose! How, out of all the possibilities, could she have come up with a name like that? It sounded like a cheap perfume, something they'd sell at one of those booths on the midway. She probably thought it was exotic; she might just as well have called herself Evening in Paris. Then he remembered the luster of her singing, and he settled back to listen.

With the opening bars, he sat up in disbelief. The silvery voice was gone and in its place was the throaty contralto of a striptease artist belting out a sticky, sentimental:

> *There's a reason for the roses that I sent you*
> *yesterday.*
> *One was red and one was yellow and like our*
> *love they fade away.*

The crowd loved it. Twisting the microphone loose, she bounded to the apron of the stage, briefly touching outstretched hands. A husky whisper came through the loudspeakers: "Kentucky Rose thanks you and just let this little ole southern gal catch her breath a minute. I just got to tune this one string on my gee-tar and . . ."

In forty-five minutes, by Joe's count, Kentucky Rose had either done wrong to or been done wrong by some no-good "cheatin' maaa-en" or else she was herself a put-upon "pore woo-man." If the first song was bad, the rest got progressively worse and the applause progressively louder. While the crowd called for yet another song the stage lights flicked off, and when they brightened again, she was gone.

Joe caught up with her in front of the food stand where they'd gone the night before. "I'll buy you a cup of coffee if you'll drop the phony southern accent."

She didn't bother to answer, but sat down at the counter and said, "I'll have a cup of coffee, Mike. Buddy-boy here is buying."

He sat down beside her. "And I'll have a hamburger with everything." He waited for her to say something, but she sat, both hands around the coffee mug, staring straight ahead.

It was stupid, he decided. Maybe she hadn't picked his pocket after all and, besides, what difference did twenty dollars make? He'd left two fifties at home on his dresser. He wasn't even hungry enough to take a bite of the hamburger. When it came, he pushed the plate to her. "Here, you eat it. I just became a vegetarian."

She did look at him then. "When did you decide that?"

"When did you decide to give yourself that idiotic name?" The minute the words were out, he knew he'd made a mistake and leaned back waiting for her to explode.

She didn't. Instead she bit into the hamburger,

chewing slowly. "I borrowed it from a girl I met once at a fair in Texas. She ended up in prison and said she wouldn't need it for a few years. Besides, it'll look good on an album cover."

"But that stuff you were singing tonight. That's not you. You're a folk singer."

"Listen, bud. You do what you have to do. Nobody's going to hand it to me on a platter. I have to earn it, and if I compromise a little to get where I'm going, so be it."

"You mean if someone just handed it to you, you wouldn't take it?"

"Sure I would, but I'd have to pay for it sooner or later. Nothing in this life is free, at least not that I've noticed. And Kentucky Rose would rather pay sooner than later." She looked up from her hamburger. "Say, speaking of paying, I thought you didn't have any money, or were you just conning me?"

"I didn't and I wasn't and I have—money, that is, enough for what you're eating." Joe pulled out the three dollar bills and laid them on the counter.

"That's fine, except the hamburger costs three bucks. That means I'm stuck for the coffee again."

"But it didn't cost that much last night."

"Of course not. Red gives me hamburgers at half price, but you ordered this one."

"How come?"

"Red's been on the same fair circuit as Henry and me for three years. We share. You should know that, being on the road and all. How long you say you've been doing this? I mean bumming around."

"Well," Joe shoved back on the bench. "To tell the truth, I just started yesterday."

"What about your folks?"

"They're—they're gone." He hid his face in his hands to keep from laughing. They would be gone, Joe was sure, if they could see him now.

He felt her hand on his shoulder. "Look. I'm sorry. It's just that you don't seem to know much on how to get along."

"I don't get it."

"I don't mean to be personal, but are those the only clothes you have?"

For a minute he couldn't answer, thinking of his walk-in closet full of more clothes than he'd ever managed to wear. "What's wrong with them?"

"Aside from the fact that you smell like a cross between a hog barn and a pancake house, nothing, but cashmere sweaters and designer jeans don't fit, somehow."

"How did you know?"

"Look, just because I don't have much money doesn't mean I'm short on taste." She stood up. "Assuming that you're telling at least part of the truth and you didn't rip them off from some local clothing store so the cops will be breathing down our necks, I'll lend you a cup of soap and thirty-five cents."

"What for?"

"For the washer and dryer. Those are machines that make clothes clean. The washer takes a quarter and the dryer, a dime." She spoke as slowly as if she were giving instructions to a preschooler. "You're too big for the monkey's costume, but maybe Henry will let you borrow a shirt and a pair of pants. Don't try to wash the sweater; cashmere has to be dry cleaned." She started walking away. "Well, come on, unless you have a better idea."

He followed her. At the moment he was fresh out of ideas.

Within the next hour, Joe learned about laundromats, the convenience of public showers, and an army cot and blanket available if you knew a certain farm kid named Ben. Kentucky Rose did.

So to keep on forgetting what he didn't want to remember, Joe Logan stayed another night at the fair.

Hogs were early risers, Joe discovered as he climbed out from under the army blanket and attempted to focus his eyes on the banner that stretched across the far end of the swine barn announcing HOGS ARE

BEAUTIFUL. Perhaps some poet or philosopher was right when he said that beauty was in the eye of the beholder, but at six in the morning, Joe's eyes weren't too capable of beholding.

Ben, the kid he'd borrowed the cot from, was already up and in the pen with a pair of pigs, answering their grunts with, "Atta girl, Agnes. Here, Stella. Glum on to this mash, you little sweetheart."

"Does it help to talk to them?" Joe sat on the edge of the cot trying to figure out where the sweetness was in a slurping Stella.

"I dunno." Ben climbed out of the pen. "But it makes me feel better. I figure I owe them something."

"And I owe you something," Joe said, "for the place to sleep. I don't have any money with me right now, but I can get some later this morning."

"No sweat." Ben leaned back against the pen. "Kind of nice to have someone to talk to besides the girls." He nodded toward the hogs. "Their vocabulary is limited. Tell you what. I have to stick around till the end of the fair, and that cot's going to be empty. The guy who was going to help me pigged out on pigs. If you can give me a hand once in a while, you can sleep for free. What do you say?"

"Thanks. I don't know for sure what I'm going to do, but if I stay, I'll need a place to sleep. But what do you mean, give you a hand? I don't know anything about pigs."

"You don't have to. Pigs don't know anything about pigs either. Are you interested?"

Joe nodded. "Okay. You show me how and I'll help you. That is, as long as I hang around. Deal?"

"Deal." Ben shook Joe's hand and turned away. "I've got to take a shower. It's me first, then Agnes and Stella. That's when I'll need you. Around ten-thirty. That okay?"

"You mean to scrub down pigs?" Joe walked over to the pen.

"Sure."

"I didn't know you washed pigs. I thought they lay around in the mud."

"These aren't ordinary pigs, my friend. They're show pigs. Purebreds. First class."

"That so?" Joe leaned over the side of the pen and looked carefully at the two animals. "They look like any other pigs to me. What makes them so special?"

"I suppose what makes anyone first class. Good breeding. Healthy environment. Good food. Tender care. You want the job?"

"Why not?" Joe grinned.

The fairground that early in the morning was enveloped in mist, with the sun showing through

like an overripe orange. It was going to be a killer—
a true Iowa "is-it-hot-enough-for-you" day that
would see the mercury shoot right past the one-
hundred-degree mark. Joe was almost sure that the
thing he wanted most to do was to go back to bed
in the cool stillness of his own house. One thing
about sleeping in a swine barn, once outside, even
the heavy air of a fairgrounds smelled fresh. He
walked through an empty midway with limp ban-
ners advertising scantily clad women, fire eaters,
snake charmers, animal freaks—promising so much
but giving so little. Those were Ashley's words,
only Ashley hadn't been talking about a midway.

He smelled coffee before he reached the line of
food booths, and when he entered the church stand,
Wanda was already there getting her kitchen in
order.

"Coffee smells good," Joe greeted her.

"He who works knows not hunger," she answered, not looking up from the bowl of pancake
batter.

"Elsie told me it was all right to come back today—to work."

"Many hands make light work." She dropped
several small dabs of batter on the griddle and
watched them sizzle and fill with tiny bubbles.

"I thought too many cooks spoil the broth." He
watched as she flipped the cakes.

"You're not cooking and there isn't any broth."

"And no dishes to wash."

"No, but here's some pancakes. At home I feed the first batch of cakes off the griddle to the dog." She flipped the cakes onto a plate and handed it to Joe.

Even though the food stand wasn't open yet, Elsie was already seated at her money table. Joe wondered briefly if she sat there throughout the entire night. She reminded him of the Picasso painting of Gertrude Stein, except she looked much less fierce.

"So you *are* back again." She didn't sound surprised. "I suppose you're going to eat and run? Well, we'll just deduct those pancakes from the money you earn, but since they look like throwaways, they'll be half price. Are you really looking for work today?"

Joe remembered reading once about Quaker Church services where the members of the congregation spoke only when the Spirit moved them. This morning, evidently, the Spirit had Elsie in a blender, for before he could answer she launched into the history of the Bear Creek Church, of the early days at the State Fair when they had to carry all their water from a water hydrant "five blocks away," of the year when the crops failed and all they cleared that year at the fair was thirty-five dollars that went to help pay the church's coal bill that next winter.

He finally finished his breakfast, and on the way back to the kitchen, he paused by Elsie's table. "I can work every day if you'd like me to. I mean if you need me."

As soon as he'd said it, he realized that it sounded like a promise he hadn't intended to make. He didn't have to keep the promise, of course; he could leave any time he wanted. He could even go home and come back any day the fair was going on. There was nothing to keep him here on the grounds. On the other hand, there was nothing to go home to, either.

Elsie folded her hands in her lap, the kind of lap that if he'd been a little kid and scared, he'd have liked to climb into and have her ward off all the threatening things of the world. "We haven't asked where you come from or where you're going," Elsie said in a soft, confidential tone. "We see you as a gift. A small gift, but still a gift. If the Spirit moves you to abide with us a little while—well, God knows best." She unfolded her hands. "In other words, yes. Eight dollars a day and food. You'd better get started, then, with the dishes."

By midmorning, he was sure he had washed more dishes in the sweat that kept running across his forehead and dripping off his nose than in the suds of his washtub. He picked up the five dollars he had coming from Elsie for his work yesterday and hurried over to the pig barn to help Ben.

He stopped just before entering the pavilion. What was Joel Wendell Logan III doing helping some dumb farm kid, who probably hadn't read a book in his life, scrub down some pigs so they could win a blue ribbon? And why was he ingratiating himself with two old farm ladies by washing dishes for his meals? Although he had to admit he had never tasted food that good: home-grown potatoes mashed with pure cream and homemade butter into a white fluff that slipped down his throat like ice cream, and roast beef . . .

He must be suffering from what Ashley would have called "upper-income guilt." At first this State Fair thing was just a game to escape for a night from being who he was, but now people were depending on him—depending on him to wash dishes and . . . pigs! He was glad his parents were gone. They would never understand. Ashley might have, but he would never be able to tell her.

"Oh, there you are," Ben called. "Thought maybe you decided not to take my offer."

"Never entered my head," Joe said hurrying down the aisle of pigs.

"Stella has manners," Ben went on, "but she

doesn't know you very well. I'll keep her steady, and you apply the shampoo and hose her off."

It wasn't difficult, really, no harder than washing his own hair in the shower; and it must have felt good to Stella because she didn't move as Joe worked the suds into her red bristles and rinsed her off again. He looked down at his hands and wondered if skin could take on a permanent pucker.

Agnes was more difficult when they took her out to the hose. Ben had to slip what looked like a hangman's noose around her neck, loop it around a post, and hold onto her hind legs.

"You must really love them," Joe said as they headed back to the barn.

"Love them? You mean the girls here? You've got to be out of your mind. The only things worse than hogs are sheep." He poked Agnes with his show cane. "Or chickens."

"I thought all farm kids loved animals. How long have you been coming here to the fair?"

Ben gave Stella a pat on her sleek back. Stella, up to her eyebrows in the feed trough, grunted her approval. "Ever since I was in grade school."

"Why? If you don't like pigs?"

Ben pulled off his cap and sat down on a bale of hay. "They're paying my way through college and law school."

"Law school!" Joel tried to imagine the wiry Ben

with his tousled, nondescript hair, off-white T-shirt, and faded bargain-basement jeans standing before a judge and arguing a case.

"Yep. I have enough saved to get me through prelaw. With luck, Agnes and Stella and their off-spring will see me through part of the rest."

"Law takes what? Six, seven years?"

"Something like that, but you'd be surprised how hogs multiply."

Joe studied the two pigs, side by side at the feed trough like twin red humps. "How many do you think it will take for law school?"

"Never really figured it out." Ben laughed. "Let's see. It takes ten bushels of corn to fatten a hog for market. If the price of corn hangs down around a buck and a half, and if hog prices stay above fifty, and if the rest of the hog raisers drop out . . ."

"Sounds like a lot of *if*'s."

"That's what farming is. All *if*'s." Ben looked up as if reading numbers from the barn rafters. "A fellow might stand to make a hundred dollars per pig. Of course, by the same token, he could lose that much just as easily if the markets go bad."

Ben sounded as if he were quoting from his father, which Joe thought he probably was. "So you're going to be a piggyback lawyer." Joe meant it as a joke.

Ben did not laugh. "I don't think it hurts to want something you don't expect to get. Then if you happen to get it, it really means something." He stood up, brushed the hay from his jeans and, un-smiling, said, "You a good friend of Kentucky Rose?"

"Me?" Joe tried not to laugh. "I never saw her before yesterday. She bought me a cup of coffee is all."

"Oh." Ben watched Agnes nose Stella out of the feed trough. "Did you ever hear her sing?"

"Yes. Over at the park. She's good."

"You bet she's good. And she deserves a break. She'll make it, though. She's like Stella here. She knows who she is. Look at Stella. See? Just the way she moves, she knows already she's going to win a blue ribbon tomorrow."

Joe watched Stella, her back a perfect crescent from snout to tail, poised like an overblown bal-lerina on her four tapering legs. He had to admit there was an air of inner confidence about her. "I see what you mean. All Stella needs is a guitar."

To his relief, Ben laughed this time. At least he felt sure of a cot and blanket for another night at the fair, if he wanted it.

Joe sweated through tubs full of dirty dishes at his noon stint in the Quaker ladies' stand, with Clyde, his chair tilted back against a tent pole, watching the women bustle by. "Son, you'd better take a breather before you melt right down into your soap suds and we lose you altogether."

"Will do," Joe hurriedly agreed.

"Better take it easy out there in that sun, too. It's a real hay burner. Fellow's likely to sun stroke if he ain't careful."

He'd take it easy, all right. He'd go home. Nothing was worth facing another tubful of dirty dishes. He stepped out of the shade of the church stand. Clyde was right. It was a hay burner. Anyone with good sense would be locked in behind a bank of air conditioners rather than trying to hide out at a state fair.

His mind made up, he headed for the gate, keeping in the shade of the grandstand. His shirt stuck to his back and clung to his armpits; his sweater hung like a limp towel from his waist and slapped at the back of his legs at every step. Around him the fair visitors pushed past, blocking the sidewalk, spilling out into the street, perspiring, red-faced and determined to find the one spot on the grounds that they'd come to the fair to see.

The screams and music from the midway collided with the smell of popcorn and charcoaled meat. He half turned, ready to head back to the relative coolness of Ben's fans in the hog barn. He'd even share them with Stella and Agnes. Almost anything would be better than shoving his way through this crowd. Then he felt a sudden coolness as if he'd stepped in front of an air conditioner. It was the Old Mill. Sure! He'd passed it that first night. It was one of the permanent attractions of the fair, not like the rides on the midway that went with the traveling carnies.

Only a couple of people were standing in line as small rowboats bobbed up and down in the narrow canal leading into a darkened cave. The rush of water that carried the boats, all linked together, into the darkness sounded as if it were rushing down a mountainside, not being stirred by some electric generator. A scratchy recording of the Beatles singing "We All Live in a Yellow Submarine" pulsed forth. He almost turned away.

Instead, Joe bought a ticket and stepped, alone, into the last boat. The vessels jerked, the water sloshed, and then they moved slowly through the mouth of the phony cave into the blackness.

The air was damp and musty, but all the noise of the fairgrounds disappeared, the only sound the faint clanking of chains beneath the shallow water. On either side and from above, fake rock walls lit here and there with blue bulbs glistened through the dark. Even the outlines of the people in the boats ahead merged with the shadows. For the first time since he'd come to the fair he was alone, and it was a different kind of aloneness than the one that waited for him at home.

The ride ended with a creak and a jangle and a scraping of wood against wood. Joe made no move to leave.

"As far as she goes, Sailor Boy." A hulk of a man, with a head that dropped off into shoulders without bothering to make a neck, stood leaning over Joe.

"I'll have some more tickets." Joe pulled the rest of his five dollars from his pocket and handed the bills to the man. "Let me know when I've used this up."

"What's with you, kid? Something down there I don't know about?"

"Yeah. Water. And it's cool."

The hulk grinned. "Okay. Let me know if you get seasick."

The chain of boats filled with more passengers and then creaked and ground down into the cave depths again. In spite of the darkness, Joe closed his eyes. Ashley used to say it was dangerous to close your eyes in the dark because you couldn't tell whether they were open or shut and you might sleep all night with your eyes open and not know it. Ashley's logic was often illogical.

"I'm scared," came a little cry from one of the boats ahead.

"Shh," some mother answered. "Be brave."

The voices softened as the boats moved slowly through the darkness. Then other voices crowded in upon him again. *His mother stood at the foot of his bed. "Do you have any idea where Ashley is? Her mother called. She's not home."*

"She's not home?" he repeated, trying to make some sense of what he thought was a bad dream.

"Did you see her today?"

All he could see of his mother was a silhouette against the hall light. "Sure. In school."

"After school, Joel?"

It wasn't a bad dream. He was awake now. "I saw her leave. In her car. I waved. She waved back. Why? What's wrong?"

"She hasn't come home, and it's almost two. They're going to notify the police."

Oh, Ashley! If he could just forget. If he could just quit remembering. If he could just come up with the right question, he might find the answer.

When he finally climbed out of the little boat, he wondered what Elsie would say if she knew he had squandered his five dollars on a kid's ride into a make-believe underground cave. He waited in line at the public showers and once inside combined his bath and laundry in one process, standing in his skivvies and shirt, then strolling back to the pig pavilion, bare-chested, his wet shirt slung over his shoulder.

"I have an extra T-shirt, if you want to borrow it," Ben said, perched up on the railing of the girls' pen.

"I sure could use one," Joe answered. "Do you spend all your time hanging around this place?"

"Most of it. I have to be here in case some breeder is interested in my girls. Good advertising. Where do you spend your time?"

Joe pulled on the T-shirt. It smelled clean like country air. "You wouldn't believe it if I told you, but I wash dishes for a Quaker church food stand. Breakfast, lunch, dinner. Get my meals and spending money. It's not much, but it's enough."

He couldn't believe what he had just said.

"Well," Ben slipped down from the railing, "they say that's how you get along in this world: cut your wants down to your needs. You going to be staying around here for a few minutes? I have to go over and get the schedule for tomorrow's showing."

The afternoon heat flowed through the swine barn as fair goers straggled past, peering into the pen as they sucked on slush cones. All the fans in the building, brought from exhibitors' homes along with the hogs, were aimed at the animals, which for the most part lay flat on their sides, eyes closed.

"So what am I doing here?" Joe asked as he leaned over the rail and scratched Stella's ear. She didn't bother to open her eyes, and he couldn't think of an answer to his own question. It was so incredibly stupid, on this hottest day of the summer, to be sitting on a bale of straw, wearing a borrowed T-shirt when he could be . . . "Doing what?" he asked Agnes. She ignored him too.

"Okay, I'll tell you," he went on, thinking that pigs were probably easier to talk to than people. "I could be at the country club. I could be at home in the pool. I could be on the phone making a date for tonight. I could be at the lake with Mom and Dad." He stopped. It was a stupid list and nothing on it was any more important than sitting and waiting until it was time to go back to greasy pans and hot soapsuds. And what difference did it make, when the one thing that could have made the difference was long gone in some underground darkness where there were no yellow submarines, no blue lights, no sloshing water?

He'd give up and go home. He'd give up looking for some crazy lost magic that never did exist. When Ben returned to relieve him of his pig-sitting duties, he'd leave.

"Stella shows at eleven. Agnes at two. And thanks a lot, Joe."

"That's okay. And good luck. Hope they win."

He couldn't care less and his words sounded that way. "See you around."

"Sure," Ben replied, as if he didn't care either.

Joe strolled down through the midway and headed toward the gates again. Of course, if he went home now he would never know if Agnes and Stella won their blue ribbons; and what would Wanda do in the kitchen without him during the evening rush? Maybe he'd go home later that night. Or, maybe, to kill time, he'd go over to the horse pavilion and watch the show. When he was a kid that was the only part of the State Fair he knew existed.

It had taken a while, but he'd finally proved to his mom that he was not cut out to jump a reluctant hunter over fake hedges in a show ring. Ashley had been a natural at it, though. He could see her now, sitting tense and unsmiling on her thoroughbred, awaiting her turn, and later, when she collected the blue ribbon for her performance, cantering around the arena with all the class of a true professional, not once changing expression, as if she were merely collecting what had been rightfully hers from the beginning.

He couldn't go any farther. He couldn't take the familiar diagonal walkway up the hill and around the twin canna beds that flanked the ornate entry to the show horse pavilion. Now was too soon, even if earlier had been too late. Ashley and her love affair with horses—or was she in love with winning?

"How do you do it? Win every time?" he remembered asking her once.

"Before I enter the ring, I hug my horse's neck and say, 'Tuck your head and don't look back.' "

He never knew whether she intended the advice for herself or the horse.

He stood undecided in the middle of the sidewalk while people pushed past. They, at least, knew where they were headed. He didn't.

"You have a new shirt!"

Someone grabbed his arm and pulled him around. In her brief cut-offs and halter she looked more like a catalogue copy of a farmer's daughter than a Kentucky Rose.

"It's Ben's. I borrowed it," Joe said, trying to get back into the character he was pretending to be. "How come you're not miming? I guess that's what a mime does, isn't it? Miming?"

"Too hot." She sighed.

"For the monkey or you?"

"For Henry. I'm free for the rest of the afternoon. Besides, you owe me for the laundry. What'll we do?"

He tried to think of something clever to say but he couldn't figure the girl out. "What do you want to do?" he offered, knowing that anything on the fairgrounds took money, and he'd just spent his last dime on a kid's ride.

"Something to cool off."

"Don't think there's a pool on the grounds, and whatever we do I'll have to get some more money from Elsie. I'm broke."

"Again!" She laughed. "And who's Elsie?"

"She's my boss. No. Wanda's my boss. Elsie's my paymaster. I have a job. Washing dishes at the Quaker Church food stand."

"Now that's a perfectly honorable profession. But never mind about the money." She skipped to catch up to his stride. "I'll treat you. I know just the place. Guaranteed to be the coolest spot on the grounds, barring none."

She pushed him through the crowd, then took his hand and pulled him off the sidewalk, across the park, and over to the Old Mill. Before he could explain that he'd spent the better part of the afternoon there, she had purchased tickets and was moving toward the entry. The same hulk of a man was taking the tickets. Joe tried to hurry by, but the man grinned a welcome. "Back again, Sailor Boy?"

Kentucky Rose quickly commandeered a boat. A chattering group of kids all wearing blue T-shirts announcing them as Coon Valley Valiants surged past, crawling like insects over the remaining boats while a wearied chaperone slumped down on a park bench. With a creak and a groan, now familiar to Joe, they all moved into the darkness of the Old Mill amid the shrieks and squeals from the not-so-valiant Valiants, but as the dark enveloped them, the voices dropped to muted whispers.

"Funny, isn't it," Joe said, "what darkness does."

"It's because dark takes away one of your senses and you get disoriented." It was an Ashley answer and coming from a Kentucky Rose it didn't make sense.

The dark didn't have that effect on the Coon Valley Valiants, however. Even before the dusty blue lights came into view, a thin little soprano started up:

> *Down by the Old Mill stream,*
> *Where I first met you.*

All the other sisters and brethren of the Coon Valley Valiants quickly joined in:

> *With your eyes so blue,*
> *Dressed in gingham too.*

Kentucky Rose could not resist:

> *It was there I knew*
> *That I loved you true,*

harmonizing an obligatto as her voice soared through the water tunnel.

> *I was sixteen. Your village queen*
> *Down by the Old Mill stream.*

"Don't you know the song?" Kentucky Rose asked.

"I've heard it, but I never listened to the words." And he hadn't.

Once through was not enough for the Coon Valley Valiants. Again the leader somewhere up the line started the song:

> *Down by the Old Mill stream,*
> *Where I first met you.*

This time Joe did join in with a tentative but tuneful baritone.

"I thought you didn't know the words," Kentucky Rose said as the last notes echoed through the cave.

"Who could miss after hearing them once?"

"I could. It takes me hours to memorize the words to a song. You must have a photographic memory."

He had always been able to do it, hear a song or

a poem once and repeat it verbatim. Thanks to Ashley and her passion for the Beatles, he could probably repeat every word they'd ever sung. "I'm not sure whether it's a talent or a curse. When remembering comes so easily, it makes forgetting awfully hard."

"That's funny. For me, remembering is harder than forgetting." She dangled one hand over the side of the boat and swished the water into miniature waves. "But I suppose it depends upon what you're trying to remember . . . or trying to forget."

"Could be."

What was he doing talking seriously to a crazy girl who kept turning up when he least expected her? Something made him want to drop his disguise and be himself again. Maybe it was the spell of the darkness, the soft ripple of the water, the feel of her shoulder against his, squeezed together as they were into the narrow seat. "Did you ever feel as if there was nothing ahead of you except week after week of solid Mondays?"

He felt her turn toward him in the dark. "I don't think I've ever been that bored! Why? Is that the way you feel?"

"Sometimes. But not so much me. Someone I knew once."

"Oh." It was more a sigh than a question.

"I think I'm beginning to know now," Joe went on, "after hanging around the fair, how she must have felt. As if life wasn't much fun anymore."

"She was a friend of yours?" she asked, not so much as if she wanted to know but more to fill in his pause.

"She was a girl with 'kaleidoscope eyes.' " His throat tightened. He couldn't go on. And why did he think it would help to put it all into words? Words couldn't begin to explain Ashley.

He was rescued by a shout from one of the Valiants, "Land ho!" and soon the darkness began to fade as the line of boats drew near an ever-widening circle of light ahead. With a sudden wrench and crunch the ride was over. Heat from the grounds flooded over them and the noises of the fair drowned out any further words. The blue lights lost their mystic charm, the water, which had rippled so softly in the cave, now became only the dirty sludge it really was, and the "village queen" of the Old Mill was only a girl he'd picked up at the fair.

"Thanks for the ride," he said. "Think I'll head for the showers. What about you?"

Kentucky Rose pushed the hair from her forehead. "Think I'll do a run-through on what I'm going to sing tonight. See you around," and she turned and was gone.

He'd lied again to her. He'd already had a shower, but it was an excuse to get away so he wouldn't have to think about Ashley.

"Joel Logan! What are you up to?"

Joe turned toward the first familiar face he'd seen in days. George Stratford. Once George had been his idol, back when Joe was a kid in junior high and George was a senior at Bradgate. George had taught him everything he knew about golf and once had even let Joe caddy for him at one of the club's tournaments.

"Bumming around. Taking in the fair. What are you doing?"

"Working. Don't I look like it?"

George didn't look like it. Compared to what Joe was wearing, George looked as if he were dressed for an executive meeting.

"I'm working for KTTV, remember? I'm out here trying to dig up some human interest stuff. That's my crew over there."

Joe turned to face a TV camera. "You're not taking footage on this, are you?"

George ruffled Joe's hair as if Joe were still the kid following him around the golf course. "I said a human interest story. You don't look too interesting and, to tell the truth, not too human. But seriously, you have any ideas? I hate to drag this crew all over, looking for a likely prospect."

"Well," Joe said, "there's a farm kid over there with two pigs named Agnes and Stella. He's showing them tomorrow for the grand championship."

"Please! No pigs! We've already done baby beeves, sheep, dogs, cats, even roosters."

"How about a monkey?" Joe laughed.

"Haven't done monkeys." George sounded half interested. "What about a monkey?"

"There's this old man with a trained monkey." Joe paused. The girl! Why not Kentucky Rose? "Listen, George, you really should look them up. This old fellow has this monkey. Then there's this mime, and everything the mime does the monkey does. It's really quite a show."

"Where's the human interest?"

"It's like this. The mime is really a girl who wants to break into country western, the big time, and she sings, for free, every night over in the park. You know that open-air stage deal?"

"She any good?" George appeared really interested now.

"She's not bad. Really, George, she's not bad."

What fun to watch old George—old George who fancied himself such a lady-killer—tangle with a carnie like Kentucky Rose. On the other hand, it'd be interesting to see how Kentucky Rose would handle George. And after all, as Ashley would say, "Why not?"

"What's her name?" George reached for a pen.

"I don't know her real name, but she calls herself Kentucky Rose."

"It figures. Well, thanks a lot, kid. I might look her up."

"Unless you'd be interested in Elsie and Wanda, who've been running their Quaker Church food stand here at the fair for the last forty years?"

"I'll try Kentucky Rose, thank you. By the way," he dabbed at his forehead with a clean, white hand- kerchief, whiter by far than Ben's T-shirt by now. "Have you . . . ?"

"Have I what?"

"Tried her? I mean, if I'm infringing . . . if she's your territory . . ."

"Look," Joe said, wanting not to understand what he was hearing. "I just met her. Just because she works at the fair doesn't mean . . ."

"Sure, Scout. I've got you. And I'll be George- Good-Guy with his magic microphone and candied camera." He motioned toward his crew. "Give me a call next week. We'll play a round of golf."

On second thought, Joe decided not to go home after all. This was better than playing a round of golf. It was "playing around with," and why not? He wasn't hurting anyone. It was like directing a cast of players who didn't know the plot and didn't even know they were being directed. He could just see Kentucky Rose. She'd probably think she'd really hit the big time if she got on local TV.

And so, Joe stayed a little longer at the fair.

❈

He was awakened the next morning by Ben tugging at him and shouting, "Wake up! Something's wrong with Agnes! You'll have to help me."

Joe scrambled off the cot, grabbed his jeans, and followed Ben. A prone Agnes, breathing in short gasps, lay on her side, feet extended.

"Heat's got her!" Ben shouted, jumping into the pen. "I called Dad and he said to load her up and bring her home. I'll bring Naomi back to take her place. I've showed her before at the County Fair."

"How's Stella?"

"She's all right."

The self-confident Stella looked up from her trough, feed dripping from her mouth, grunted once and put her snout back into her breakfast.

"How are you going to get her home?"

"I have the pickup. But you'll have to help me load her." Ben knelt beside the heaving Agnes.

"Load her? How?"

"I have the truck backed up to the chute. Come on. Give me a hand."

Together they tugged Agnes to her feet and with

Ben's arms around her neck and Joe half carrying her rear, they maneuvered the pig out of the pen, over to the chute, Agnes staggering like a drunken dowager.

"Listen, Joe," Ben said as he dropped the endgate into place. "It's a two-hour drive home and two hours back. Dad said he'd have Naomi ready. I should be back around ten-thirty. You know Stella has to be in the show ring at eleven. Could you stay around and get her ready? You know. Bathe her. Brush her. Exercise her."

"Sure. I guess so but—" Joe hesitated. "I'll have to tell Elsie. That's who pays me for washing dishes."

Ben hoisted himself up into the cab of the pickup. "It's going to be so hot anyway. Nobody's going to be hanging around a food stand today."

Ben was right. Elsie agreed no one would be ordering pancakes and coffee on such a day as this was promising to be.

"But I'll be back at noon, for sure," Joe promised. "You see, I got to help this guy with his pigs."

"You don't have to explain," Elsie said. "On a farm, pigs come first!"

With his reprieve from the breakfast dishes, Joe hurried back to the swine barn, sat down on a bale of hay, and looked at Stella, still up to her eyeballs in the feed trough.

"Well, old girl. It's you and me for the blue ribbon."

It was insane! Stuck in a stinky hog barn, getting a dumb pig ready to compete for a stupid blue ribbon. And to think that only a few days ago all he knew about a pig was a Windsor Chop or Sweet-and-Sour Pork.

He couldn't remember the order Ben had said. Was it exercise, bathe, and brush? Or bathe, brush, and exercise? He walked down the length of the pavilion and looked out. A scrawny kid was walking a white pig around. Exercise it would be.

"You may not need it, Stella, but I do," he said as he herded the pig down the alleyway, tapping her gently with a cane to guide her, the way he had seen Ben do.

Next to food, Stella loved water, preferably water turned into a puddle of mud. He had her all scrubbed down and ready to herd back to her pen when she lay down in the puddle under the hydrant, grunting at him in delight. He eventually got her out of the puddle and back into her pen. By that time, Joe was as dirty as the pig.

"All right. If that's the way you're going to act, it's a spit bath for you."

Stella backed her rear into the corner of the pen and refused to move, even when he tried to lure her with ground corn. He filled a pail with water and soap suds and attacked her with sponge and brush. The stupid pig had muscles in places he didn't even know were places on a pig.

"Give her a kick," the scrawny kid yelled from across the alley.

A kick worked. Stella moved reluctantly. He brushed her until every bristle lay like a well-kept lawn. As he crawled out of the pen he looked over at the kid again. "What are you doing now?"

"Polishing the hoofs."

Joe had never hear of polishing pigs' feet, but if it took that to keep Stella in the running, he'd do it. He did have to admit, when he finished, that Stella looked absolutely perfect—for a pig. As for himself, he looked, and felt, like a pig. A quick dash to the showers and a borrowed pair of shorts and a T-shirt from Ben's footlocker took care of that. After all, it was a small price for Ben to pay for Stella's beauty treatment.

He sat down, finally, to wait for Ben. After a while, he stood up and walked to the open doorway to wait for Ben. He turned and wandered down the long alleyway with its grunting horde of pigs to wait for Ben. He strolled out to the show ring and hung over the entry gate to wait for Ben. He turned just in time to see a line of pigs herded by an assortment of T-shirted and blue-jeaned keepers heading for the ring.

"You mean it's show time?" he asked a man guarding the gate.

"In five minutes," the man answered.

Joe rushed back to the barn. The pens were emptying. Where was Ben and how long did it take to drive home and back? Joe had spent his whole morning getting Stella ready for her showing and now, no show.

He grabbed Ben's cane, tugged open the pen, and tapping Stella gently on the rump, herded her toward the ring. "Come on old girl. Let's you and me go for broke!"

Stella waddled out like a *prima donna*, Joe following with the cane, tapping and urging her toward the entry gate. He had just succeeded in getting Stella aimed toward the show ring when someone yelled, "Hey! You in the white shorts. Isn't that a gilt you got there?"

Joe whirled around. "A guilt? Where?"

"Your pig. Isn't it a gilt?"

Joe looked down at Stella. "I don't know. Why?"

At first Joe thought the man was going to take a poke at him. "Listen, smart neck! Gilts don't show 'til eleven. Now move your dang gilt out of here!"

"Okay. Okay," Joe muttered, hurrying to negotiate Stella into a right-about-face.

Was it his imagination or did Stella sort of slink back to her pen? "Don't let it upset you, old girl.

You're no 'dang gilt.' You're one good-looking girl-pig, and don't you forget it!" He slipped Stella back into her pen, hoping no one had noticed their embarrassing expedition, brushed her down again, and dusted off her hoofs. The kid across the alley was removing his pig's feed trough and water. Joe followed suit, vowing he'd watch the kid and do whatever he did, but where was that Ben?

"When do you show?" he finally called over to the kid.

"Eleven."

The kid was showing a gilt too! Stella was home free. Now if Ben would only show up.

Ben did *not* show. When the kid herded his ugly white pig—and it was ugly compared to Stella— toward the show ring, Joe and Stella stalked them like two bloodhounds. Bleacher seats, all full, lined the circle of the show ring. He marveled that so many people could be interested in pigs. A stern-looking man wearing a white coat and clutching a clipboard eyed Stella as she ambled into the ring. Joe kept her snout on the heels of the kid ahead and when they had circled the ring twice, the kid stopped. Joe managed to stop Stella too.

The judge moved down the line of competing pigs, eyeing each animal from all angles. Joe noticed how the kid readied his pig for inspection, so when the judge reached Stella, Joe tapped her back legs with the cane, and Stella, as if on cue, stretched out so that her entire formation was readily visible. The judge stopped in front of Stella. Carefully Joe rubbed Stella's sleek belly with the tip of his cane so that she arched her back into a perfect crescent.

The man finally moved on and Joe felt his stomach relax. He reached down and patted Stella on her jowls. "Good girl. So far so good." She grunted two soft grunts in answer. At a signal from the judge or from someone, Joe didn't know who, the pig troop paraded around the ring again. Joe prayed that Kentucky Rose had been right that circles brought good luck, but he need not have worried. Stella maneuvered the ring as if she were smelling out a blue ribbon of truffles. The crowd grew suddenly quiet, and Joe felt for the first time the hundreds of eyes looking down at him. The white coat approached Joe again. "Walk around again, son."

"Alone?"

"Well, with your pig, of course," the judge answered with a puzzled glance from Stella to Joe.

Shakily, Joe tapped Stella along her solo waddle around the ring, the judge studying her as if he'd never seen a pig before. Finally the man pointed to a spot in the center of the assembled pigs. Joe coaxed Stella up to the indicated spot, and before his cane had even touched her nose, she stopped as if on command. The man knelt beside Stella, feeling her shanks, rubbing his hand across her back, gazing into her eyes, patting and probing her sides, and then, with a flourish, he whipped out a blue ribbon and slapped it on Stella's back. The crowd broke out in applause.

Joe dropped to his knees, wrapped both arms around Stella's front, and buried his face in her bristles. "We did it, Stella! Who said circles weren't lucky! We did it!" Never before had he felt such joy at winning. He had showed a pig to a blue ribbon at a State Fair. It was unbelievable! It was pure magic!

A whistle cut through the air. Joe looked up into the bleachers, and there, on the top row, was Ben, waving his cap and shouting something Joe couldn't hear. Ashley would have died laughing if she could have seen him on his knees in the sawdust of a show ring, hugging a pig!

⚓

He gladly turned over Stella, the cane, and the blue ribbon to a grateful Ben, who looked as proud as Joe felt. "A real class act, Joe. You're a natural with pigs, you know. Maybe you should show Naomi for me this afternoon."

"No, thanks. I think I'll quit while I'm ahead." Joe closed the pen's gate as Stella gave up her stardom in favor of food. "Besides, Stella's kind of like Kentucky Rose. As you said, one of a kind, I mean."

"Yeah, she's an original all right." Ben carefully hung the blue ribbon on the side of the pen. "Tell you what. Tomorrow's the last day of the fair, but I won't be taking the girls home till later. Why don't you and Kentucky Rose and me do the fair tonight after she gets through singing. I'll even pay."

"Sounds good," Joe said. "I guess I might as well hang around. But I'll split whatever it costs. You're saving money for law school, remember."

Ben leaned against a stack of hay bales and looked serious. "I know it's none of my business, but haven't you thought about going to college? There are scholarships available and you can always get a job of some kind—like washing dishes."

"You really think so?" Joe tried to keep his face straight. What would Ben think if he knew that what Joel Wendell Logan III received every month from his grandfather's trust fund was enough to buy Stella, Agnes, Naomi, and all their relatives?

"Sure. And listen," Ben went on. "Dad and I couldn't offer you much for wages and board and room, but if you wanted to stick around through September, we could use some help during fall farrowing."

Joe had no idea what *farrowing* entailed, but figured it must have something to do with pigs. "Let me think about it." Avoiding Ben's eyes, he gazed down the alleyway to the HOGS ARE BEAUTIFUL banner. "Besides, first we have to do the fair. Right?"

"Do the fair!" As Joe attacked the stacks of coffee mugs, pie plates, silverware, pots, and pans—as he washed, rinsed, and piled with the regularity of a robot—he thought about "doing the fair." It was a funny expression. In high school, kids were always talking about "doing" drugs, "doing" sports, "doing" sex. It made everything sound like some kind of obligation or duty. It never sounded like fun.

As he left the food stand, Joe remembered what he'd said earlier about quitting while he was ahead. He wondered, before he could stop himself, if that was what Ashley had thought. Then without any planning, with no conscious decision, he was through the main gates of the fairgrounds and in a taxi headed for home.

The cabbie was skeptical until he heard the address and even then was doubtful until Joe produced his house key. Whether it was the key itself or the monogram or the gold holder that convinced him, Joe wasn't sure and didn't care.

The half-hour drive didn't seem long enough to account for the sensation of stepping from one world into another. After the noise and heat and smells and dust of the fair, the carefully tended lawn and the shaded coolness of the house where he'd spent his entire life seemed alien, not familiar. The driver walked with him to the door, and only after seeing that the key actually fit the lock, returned to his cab to wait to be paid.

Joe was shoving the change from the fare back into his pocket and closing the door when the silence of the house surrounded him. He stood for a moment, his hand still on the doorknob, and felt the quiet wrap itself around him. He was alone—totally, completely, absolutely alone.

Everything was exactly as he'd left it. How many nights ago? His parents were still at the lake, the maid was still on vacation, the air was still at precisely the correct degree of coolness. Nothing had changed, yet Joe felt like an intruder.

Slowly he climbed the broad staircase, pausing for a moment on the second floor to listen to the silence, then moving on to the third floor. He stood again in the doorway, looking at his room with the eyes of a stranger. He'd never thought before about how much space there was. His bathroom was the size of Elsie's Quaker food stand, the bedroom with its fireplace and den would have held a dozen Stellas and their offspring. He looked down at his shirt. Ben's shirt, really. A bit of straw still clung to the sleeve.

After he'd showered and changed to his swim trunks, he punched on the answering machine attached to his phone. A couple of invitations to parties, a friend who wanted to set up a tennis date, a call from the clothing store to tell him the sports jacket he'd ordered was ready to be picked up, Ashley's mother inviting him to lunch . . . and George, who'd phoned to thank Joe for Kentucky Rose. It sounded, as he turned off the machine, as if George were quietly laughing at some private joke. He wondered briefly how he could have forgotten how much he'd grown to dislike George.

He hurried through the hall, down the stairs. It was not just the absence of noise that made the silence so heavy. It was more as if he'd slipped into a time warp, where things had gone awry, where the days at the fair never had existed, where it had been only an hour or two since he'd seen his parents off to the lake. He tried to whistle, but the crazy Beatles tune that came was one he didn't want to remember.

He detoured through the kitchen on his way to the pool. Somehow between Stella and dishwashing, he'd skipped not only breakfast but lunch as well. He patted the automatic dishwasher on his way to the refrigerator. There was plenty of food, of course, but, he thought as he looked at the loaded shelves, nothing to eat. Cheese from Brie through

Maytag to Stilton, patés, California figs, Australian kiwis, New Zealand uglis, prosciutto and Smithfield ham—all of it looking like a photograph in *Gourmet*, none of it right, somehow.

The water of the pool glistened in the afternoon sunlight, clear and bright. The light reflecting from the blue and white tiles made him squint as he balanced on the end of the diving board. He liked to dive. There was always a scant second at the peak of the arc when, poised in midair, he felt completely free of everything. Then came the water roaring past his ears as he sliced through the surface, the water streaking over his body and then the clear, clean bubbles rising with him to the top.

Over and over, he repeated the dive, the brief swim to the side of the pool, then another dive. Dive, swim, climb, dive: action took the place of thought until finally, after how long Joe wasn't sure, he threw himself, panting, on a chaise longue.

The bright water of the pool continued to slap against the tiled wall, and he stared until the pool's surface became as still as a mirror.

"Where is she?" he had asked when his mother turned *from the phone that bleak November morning.*

"The fairgrounds," she said, her voice as pale as her *face. "In a parking lot near the horse pavilion."*

Now, after months of futile questions, the answer was still beyond reason, beyond comprehension to anyone but Ashley. "Why?" he shouted in the harsh sunlight of the August afternoon. "Why?"

The sound of his own voice forced him to his feet, sent him almost running through the silent house, up the stairs to his bedroom where the shorts and shirt he'd borrowed from Ben lay crumpled on the floor.

"Why didn't you tell me?" he shouted again, this time without saying the words aloud.

The strength of his anger and the utter emptiness of the house paralyzed him for a moment. Then slowly, feeling like an old man, he stripped off the swim trunks and dressed again in Ben's clothes.

There was nothing here, only questions, with silence for an answer. He would go back. Joe would stay another night at the fair.

❧

He parked the car in the long-term lot, locked his wallet in the trunk, and shoved a fifty-dollar bill in his shoe, his *left* shoe. Kentucky Rose would have approved. "Left is lucky," she'd informed him, "it's the heart side. That's why I always hold the mike in my left hand when I'm singing a capella."

As Joel hurried through the midway, he glanced at the area where Henry and the mime and the monkey would go through their routines when the evening crowd began to arrive. George's TV crew was busy setting up, but George was nowhere in sight. Probably putting the make on Kentucky Rose, Joe thought with a twinge of guilt, but she was old enough to take care of herself.

Nothing had changed at the food tent either, he decided, as Wanda handed him a brand-new scouring pad and said, "Try to make this last through tomorrow. Waste not, want not."

The familiar dishwashing routine was as effective in blotting out thinking as diving into the pool. For a little while at least, nothing was more important than scouring the last bit of grease from the corner of a pan or making sure there was no stain left in the bottom of the coffee cups.

It was time to "do" the fair. Joel picked up part of his pay from Elsie with a "Save the rest. I'll be back tomorrow," and wondered when tomorrows had become so important.

The heat of the day still hung like a muggy mist over the grounds as he sat down beside Ben in front of the open-air stage.

"You showed up after all," Ben said. His voice was flat and tight. He didn't look at Joe; instead he leaned forward and stared at the stage where a bunch of kids were skipping rope more or less in time with an off-stage record blaring through the sound system.

"After all what?" Joe asked. It was like talking to a stranger. Maybe Naomi hadn't lived up to expectations.

"After all the crap you've been pulling. Poor old Joe. No last name. No family. Washing dishes. Showing a dumb pig for a farm kid even dumber."

"What are you talking about?" It wasn't flatness he was hearing now, it was disgust.

"The game you've been playing with us. Joel Logan III. That name Logan is plastered all over the city: Logan Building, Logan Bank, Logan Zoo. What were you trying to pull? A little sociological experiment on how the bottom half lives? I can tell you one difference—that half doesn't lie."

"It wasn't an experiment." Joe felt something he couldn't name, something he'd never felt before. He wondered if it were called shame.

"So it *was* a game. Or maybe a bet?"

"Look, I was just trying to be someone else for a change. What's wrong with that?"

"Depends on where you start. It's pretty easy to slip down for a few days and be a nobody. Don't you know it takes years for a nobody to work up to a somebody?"

"What difference does it make? What do you care?"

"I care because you made me feel like an idiot. I

meant it about the job. We could have used your help. I thought you were real. I thought I could trust you."

The jump rope act slithered off the stage and the emcee bounced on.

"How did you find out?"

Ben pointed to the stage where Kentucky Rose stood.

"But how did she—?"

Applause drowned out his question.

"She's wearing Stella's ribbon," Joe shouted in Ben's ear. "How come?"

Ben was standing, clapping with the rest of the crowd. "It was supposed to be a surprise for you. It turned out to be a joke on us."

The sound of Kentucky Rose's voice, the sound Joe had heard that first night at the fair, quieted the audience.

> *Oh dear, what can the matter be?*
> *Oh dear, what can the matter be?*
> *Oh dear, what can the matter be?*
> *Joe, he's so long at the fair.*

Throughout the rest of the song, the rest of the performance, Ben did not talk. Kentucky Rose did not look in their direction. Joe glanced away from the stage. George's television crew was set up, cameras trained on Kentucky's face.

"They're filming it!"

"Of course they are," Ben said. "He's a friend of yours, isn't he? Or do the Logans own the TV station too?"

"That's how you found out, wasn't it?"

"Kentucky Rose'll tell you, if she's still talking to you, which I doubt."

What were they so angry about? He'd won a blue ribbon for Ben. He'd given Kentucky Rose TV exposure. And there was nothing phony about those dishes he'd washed. He hadn't lied; he just hadn't told them everything. Ashley always claimed that wasn't lying. There she was again! Everything led back to Ashley.

Kentucky Rose finished her act and left the stage. Ben, without a word, stood up and hurried over to where George and his crew were gathered around Kentucky. Joe started toward them, then stopped. How could he explain to them things he could not understand himself? It was crazy. He'd come to the fair to escape being Joel Wendell Logan III, to escape remembering, to escape the questions that Ashley had left unanswered. He knew if he were to find those answers, he'd have to start at the beginning.

He'd see Ben and Kentucky Rose later. First, as always, there was Ashley.

He walked up the hill to the horse pavilion. The show was over, the building empty as he climbed slowly to the top row of the arena. All the lights were off, and through the open windows of the circular dome, the sounds of the fair drifted. In the semi-darkness, he looked down at the tanbark of the show ring and let himself remember what he had tried for months to forget.

PART III

❦

Ashley and Me

"The trouble with you, Ashley," I said, "is that you make life too difficult. Just live it. Don't dissect it, which is what we're supposed to be doing to this stupid frog."

"That's just the point, Joel." She nudged the frog with her pencil. "Why are we supposed to be taking a frog apart?"

"To see how it works, I guess."

"I think this frog is premanently broken. Besides, I don't care how he works, do you?" Her voice was quietly fierce.

Ashley was an irresistible force. Unfortunately, the objects she met proved to be immovable. In fifth grade she sent a letter to the President of the United States protesting zoos.

"Animals should not be caged up like animals," she wrote. All she got back for an answer was a smiling photograph of the President, autographed. The next day she staged a one-person hunger strike in front of the bear's cage in Logan Park Zoo. Her demonstration lasted exactly two hours, with the TV cameras taking miles of footage of her before her mother arrived and scooped her off the path.

Her family finally bought her a horse and started her in on riding lessons, thinking that would get her through the animal phase, but in sixth grade, it was save the seals. In seventh grade, it was whales, and by the time she got to eighth grade her causes included all fur-bearing animals and endangered species. I got used to seeing her picture in the paper, but her protests didn't do any good. Our parents still bought fur coats and contributed tax-deductible grants to Logan Park Zoo.

Her parents would have sent her to a prep school the next year if the closest one hadn't been over a thousand miles away. The Midwest wasn't big on prep schools, but Bradgate was a close equivalent.

Ashley and I were partners in biology lab that freshman year at Bradgate High. With microscopes ready, we had aimed at amoebas and peered at parameciums, but on the day devoted to dissecting angleworms, Ashley deliberately missed school, not because she was a sissy, but because, she said, "it was killing without a reason! It's not like we're going to eat it or something. That would make sense, but all we're going to do is cut it up and draw pictures of it when there are perfectly good pictures in the book!"

Then came frogs.

The frog, of course, wasn't alive. It was pickled. I'd fished ours out of the big jar on Mr. Hawley's desk and laid in on our cutting board while Ashley stood back and looked at me in horror.

"Murderer!" she said.

"I didn't kill it. It's already dead. Now hand me some pins."

Instead, she covered the frog with our lab manual and stared out the window. "How can you do it? He looks just like Kermit!"

"All frogs look alike," I said, uncovering the frog.

"And he looks a little bit like Mr. Hawley." She shuddered.

I laughed. "You're crazy, you know."

"No. But I'll tell you what I do know." She rested her hand on my arm. Ashley was a toucher. It was as if she couldn't trust just words to work for her but had to reach out and feel to see if I understood. "Being with you is like being alone."

"Thanks a lot," I said, grabbing up the pins. "You sure know how to hurt a guy."

She looked at me, almost startled. "Don't you see? That's a compliment. Anything so comfortable should be completely boring, but I'm never bored with you."

I forgot about the frog and concentrated on Ashley. "It figures. You're never bored with me because it's like being by yourself."

"You're talking in circles. And you, Joel Logan, have about as much intuition as a mole. Not everything has to be put into words." She picked up the lab manual and placed it again like a tent over our frog, and walked to the window. "Do you know sometimes trees—particularly in fall—are so beautiful it makes you hurt?"

"Maybe you're a Druid at heart and don't know it."

She pretended not to hear me.

"Did you ever wonder where the now ends and the then begins?"

"Never!" I said, uncovering the amphibian and thinking for the hundredth time that trying to follow an Ashley conversation was like playing hopscotch with a cricket.

"It must happen between the clicks of seconds," she went on.

"Between the clicks of seconds," I repeated, opening the manual to the illustration of what the frog was supposed to end up looking like. "There's probably a name for it."

"Maybe it's the same as the space between lightning and thunder."

"Time lapse," I muttered, picking up another handful of pins.

"Time *is* a lapse. Time sucks!"

I dropped the pins. Ashley was chewing on her bottom lip and staring out the window again.

"That'd make a good song." I picked up the pins again. "Time laps when I'm with yo-oo-ou," I sang in a nasal falsetto. "Time sucks when I leave yo-oo-ou."

Ashley turned, smiled a nothing smile, came over beside me, and stared down at our frog. "Look at his little mouth! Do you know that our tongues are hinged at the back of our mouths rather than at the front like frogs'?"

"No, but if we expect to pass biology, we've got to get started. Here, stick a pin in here, will you?"

"No! I will not. And who says I have to?"

"They do." Out of the corner of my eye I saw Mr. Hawley starting his round of inspection.

"Who are they?"

"Right now, 'they' is Mr. Hawley."

"Did you call me?" Mr. Hawley loomed over us. Ashley was right. He did look vaguely like our frog.

"A little squeamish, are we?" he said laughing. Before either of us could move, he picked up a handful of pins and with four precise jabs had the frog firmly fixed to our cutting board. Then smiling at Ashley, he reached for the knife and slashed the frog neatly open from chin to whatever you call the opposite end of a frog. "Now then," he said, beaming. "Carry on." And he handed the scalpel to Ashley.

It took Mr. Hawley a couple of seconds to realize that Ashley was not going to take the knife. Instead she just stood there, looking down on the frog and shaking her head.

"I know," Mr. Hawley went on, wiping his hand against his lab coat, "it's asking quite a bit of the girls in this class to dissect a frog just before lunch period, but if you wish, you can come in after school and . . ."

"It's not that," Ashley interrupted. "It's that we're breaking a chain. A chain of life, and everything depends on everything else and when you take out one link, no matter how small it is, then you've wiped out something that nobody can ever put back again."

"But, Ashley." Mr. Hawley half laughed. "It's only a frog. Besides, you're not killing it. I didn't kill it. It's already dead. All you have to do is cut it up so you can see how it lived."

"That's like saying," Ashley persisted, "that you're not sure anything's alive until after it's dead. Besides, it doesn't really matter who does the killing. What matters is the reason."

"Now, Ashley," Mr. Hawley explained carefully, "you realized when you enrolled in this class that one of the requirements was to dissect a frog. I can't see how I could possibly give you a passing grade if you refuse to perform the required tasks."

"I could read about frogs instead. How they lived."

"But, Ashley." His voice dropped. "You know as well as I that if I were to break the rules for you I'd have to do the same for everyone in this class. You can see that, can't you?"

Ashley shrugged. "It'd sure save a lot of frog lives, wouldn't it?"

Mr. Hawley's mouth opened as if he were going to say something, but instead he turned and moved on to the next table.

I looked at Ashley, whose jaw was set in what I knew was pure stubbornness. "So you'd rather flunk than slice? You know, don't you, that's stupid."

She frowned at the impaled frog. "Well, how would *you* feel if you were out there somewhere eating flies and sunning yourself on a nice muddy bank and then . . . Wham! . . . Pow! . . . Gone!"

"I'm not sure frogs feel," I muttered as I picked up the knife.

Ashley turned her back and spent the rest of the hour gazing out the window. The bell finally rang. I stayed after school to finish off our frog and Ashley galloped off to her riding lesson, but the next day she dropped the course and switched to what she called "Remedial Science." The kids watched nature movies instead of dissecting frogs; the football coach ran the projector and for a little while Ashley stopped making waves. I wondered how long *that* would last.

If you didn't know Ashley, it woud be hard to take her seriously. She certainly didn't look like a crusader. She looked more like a stray pixie with her short haircut, her eyes that never stayed the same color but changed from blue to green to hazel depending on what was going on in her head, and something always was. Ashley gave off a kind of warmth controlled by a thermostat that only Ashley understood. When we were together, doing even the most everyday kinds of things, I always felt special. She had the same effect on everyone else, too. She wasn't particularly pretty, but she had what adults always call "good bones."

She also had all the money she'd ever need, more than she could ever spend. We shared that condition, Ashley and I—the money—thanks to our grandfathers who, between them, had owned most of the city. If we had any problem at all it was that neither of us needed to work for anything. We had it all.

Our parents had known each other for years, although it seemed to me the only things they realled shared were their backgrounds. To tell the truth, Ashley's parents were a bit hard to like, but Mom and Dad didn't seem to notice.

Of course, you couldn't really classify Ashley. Other kids were guys or girls, jocks, creeps, nerds, or brains. Ashley was . . . Ashley.

I knew that for sure by the time I was ten. Mom said I could ask anybody I wanted to my birthday party. I invited all the guys in my class—and Ashley.

"You can't do that," Mom insisted. "Ashley won't come if she's the only girl. Her mother won't let her, I'm sure."

Mom was wrong. Ashley came, but she didn't give me a present until all the other kids had left.

We were sprawled on towels out by the pool, drying off in the sun when she pulled the package out of her beach bag. I laughed because it was typical Ashley. Instead of fancy paper and big bows, it was wrapped carefully in newspaper, and fastened with stickers from Greenpeace.

Before she handed it to me, she made me sit up and face her. "And you've got to swear," she said looking so serious that I wanted to giggle, "that you will never, ever just stick this in a whole pile of records on the stereo. It has to be played all by itself, or you'll lose the magic."

I swore and crossed my heart because I knew that Ashley was perfectly capable of un-giving a present. I couldn't see what the big deal was, but I was curious and besides, I didn't want to hurt her feelings if she thought it was important. I was even careful about unwrapping it.

When I looked up, Ashley was grinning so hard I thought her face would break. "Isn't it magnificent? It's never even been played. See, the jacket is still taped shut."

I looked back down again, trying to figure out what to say. "Wow. This has to be an antique." It wasn't much, but it was the best I could do. What else could I say about a Beatles album that was dated 1967?

"It's not an antique, Joel. It's a classic. See, all the lyrics are on the back and all the people on the cover are wax. From Madame Tussaud's. That's in London."

"*Sgt. Pepper's Lonely Hearts Club Band,*" I read. "Hey, this is weird." It was, because the faces on the jacket looked real, but they were all scrambled together, some of them really old, like a hundred years ago, and some of them belonged to people I'd seen on television in late, late movies. "Where'd you get it?"

"There's a place in Chicago where you can get all sorts of stuff like that by mail. It's for serious collectors. I read about it in a magazine. But come on. Don't you want to hear it?" She tugged me to my feet and by the time we got to my bedroom, I'd heard a mini-history of all four Beatles with special emphasis on John Lennon, who, Ashley assured me, was a kind of super-Beatle.

I wasn't crazy about the music at first, but after we'd listened to it about five times, I began to see why Ashley was excited. It was kind of like being in the middle of some crazy traveling circus with everything going on at the same time. She had the words memorized, and it didn't take me long to remember most of them, so we spent the rest of my birthday afternoon sitting on the floor and singing along with the recording.

For the next seven years, on my birthday I always knew what kind of present Ashley would give me and we always spent those afternoons in the same way. I was the only one she shared her collecting with because she was my friend.

For the same reason, I was the only person she ever lied to. That may sound crazy, but sometimes the truth really hurts and Ashley would rather lie than hurt me.

There was this girl, Carla, in junior high who was very popular. She had long, blond hair that sort of swept down over her shoulders and she usually wore bright yellow sweaters or blouses so you couldn't help noticing her. I don't remember her last name; in fact, I'm sure I never talked to her, but I wanted to take her to the school dance. I used to dream about her and watch her. I knew her schedule of classes and every room she was in at any hour of the day. Of course, she never noticed me because she was usually surrounded by a bunch of other guys, and I was just an eighth-grade TAG.

"Would you sort of find out, Ashley? You know, ask her if maybe she'd go with me to the dance, if I asked her?"

Ashley asked her for me, of course.

"She said . . ." Ashley's eyes changed color at least twice. "She said she'd already promised Greg Sloane, but that it was nice of you to think of her. She says you're really neat."

"Carla did?"

Carla didn't. What she really said, I learned later from some kids who were standing around and heard Ashley ask, was, "That nerd! I'd go alone first!"

When I pointed out the lie to Ashley, her eyes stayed as blue as the sweater she was wearing. "It was a nice lie, wasn't it? You know what the kids call us, don't you?"

I didn't.

"You're Mr. Perfect. But that's better than what they call me."

"I've never heard them call you anything."

"They call me 'the girl you love to hate.' "

Nobody ever called her that! She had made it up so I wouldn't feel bad about being called Mr. Perfect.

We were walking home together after that stupid dance. Our parents made us go. She had spent the night standing over on one side of the gym surrounded by a bunch of girls, and I had spent the time just inside the door watching Carla and feeling like the nerd she'd called me. I finally stopped feeling sorry for myself and started home, and that's when Ashley caught up with me.

"Know what? I discovered something! If you try hard enough, it's possible to become invisible." She stopped in the middle of the sidewalk.

I didn't stop. I kept on walking and wishing I were Greg Sloane and that Carla, instead of Ashley, were running after me.

"It's true! You can be right in the middle of a whole bunch of people and if you think hard enough, they can't even see you."

"That's dumb, Ashley. Really dumb. You're coming unglued."

She ran to catch up again and then walked backward ahead of me. "It works. It really does. I just tried it. It's kind of like watching a play rehearsal and you're way back in the theater and the actors don't even know you're around."

"So?"

"So why don't we be invisible from now on till school's over. We can pretend we're anyplace except junior high if we think hard enough. We can do it with a little help from our friends."

I'd gotten so used to her quoting from Beatles lyrics that sometimes I wasn't sure whose words were whose. "Who are our friends?" I asked.

She grinned up at me. "We are, Joel. And for the rest of this semester, we'll both live in a yellow submarine. Then we'll be in high school and we'll be free."

We did manage to stay submerged for a month and then it was summer and then we were freshmen at Bradgate High. When Ashley said we'd be free, she'd ignored the fact that graduating from Bradgate marked people for life. When an alum died, no matter how old, having been a student at the school was always included in the obituary, an item tucked in like a seal of approval. Of course, both Ashley's and my parents graduated from Bradgate.

Our TAG group remained the cream of the élite. There were no gangs, of course, but lots of little "in" groups that constantly shifted and pretended to be exclusive of each other.

I remember only a couple of things about that time, apart from the frog fiasco, though lots of things must have happened. I do know that the sophomore TAGS had a Christmas and Hanukkah gift exchange. Ashley drew my name and gave me a year's membership in Amnesty International. She had switched from saving seals and befriending frogs to protecting people and preserving Beatles. That was the same year she won a national essay contest on the role of women in the political power structure and refused to accept the prize because the judges were all men. Her mother tried to talk her out of the decision, but Ashley, as usual, won. They puzzled each other—Ashley and her mother. I don't know if they ever talked to each other about it, but Ashley said once, "Mother can't understand me. She doesn't approve of what I do. I don't approve of how she thinks. You can't love and control at the same time, can you?"

It sounded sincere, but too heavy for me to deal with, so I said the first thing that came to mind. "That's what you do with your horse, isn't it?"

"That's different." She walked away; then she came back, reached out, and took both my hands in hers. "It *is* different, isn't it?" Her hands were cold.

I didn't know how to answer. "Come on," I said. "We'll be late for class."

We were!

It must have been spring vacation that year when Ashley, who was with her mom and dad in the Bahamas, sent me a postcard. It was one of those trick photography things where the fish is twice as big as whoever is holding it.

> Hi. This is me. A fish out of water.
> Adolescence is boring but not as
> excrutiating as Bradgate. There is life
> without it, but is there life after it?

She didn't bother to sign it. I didn't bother to keep it.

When I think about that time, I feel as if I'm going in circles because that was part of knowing Ashley—like turning a kaleidoscope, like coming back to the fair, like the Ferris wheel, like the show ring in the horse pavilion. Except those kinds of circles don't have an ending or a beginning. They just continue retracing themselves, bigger or smaller or the same size. That's what my junior year at Bradgate was like.

The test paper lay on the corner of my desk, but

I didn't bother to pick it up and look at my grade. Not that I was worried. Trig was a snap, and the test had been easy, unusual for Mr. Kastner. I was really waiting for Ashley to look at her grade. It was ritual with us to see who rated higher. If I beat her, she owed me a Tom Swiftie, but I was pretty sure I was going to owe her one because she had finished the test at least fifteen minutes before I had.

Miss Jacobs had introduced our Advanced English class to Swifties, informing us that they were an "inductive method of demonstrating the overuse of adverb modifiers after attributives." She made an art of impressing us with her vocabulary, but I soon figured out how to impress her. I found a handbook on literary terms in the library, and when I started sprinkling "denouement," "prosody," and "colophon" into my themes, I was home free.

Thinking up new Swifties for Ashley, though, was not that easy. "We're *dead*locked," Tom said im*passive*ly. I used that one before. It was one of my best. "I'm *cold*," Lady Godiva said *shiftless*ly. That was Ashley's latest. I locked my eyes on Mr. Kastner as he started explaining something about the test and concentrated on Swifties. "I'm *bored*," Tom sighed w*hole*heartedly. It definitely was not up to an Ashley standard.

"I didn't make the honor *roll*," Tom sighed *list*lessly. It would have to do. I picked up my test paper and peeked at the grade. I'd missed one, but I had my Swiftie ready.

"What'd you get?" I whispered across to Ashley.

She grinned as if she'd hit the jackpot and held up her paper. A red *F* blazed from the top right-hand corner.

"You couldn't. . . ." I said, risking a quick side-long glance in her direction. "It was so easy! You . . . you did it on purpose!"

Ashley lifted her head and appeared to be engrossed in Kastner's explanation, but I could see her smile.

I ducked my head and pretended to be taking notes. "Why?"

She turned to me and without even attempting to lower her voice practically shouted. "Why not?"

Mr. Kastner stepped out in front of his podium. "Did you have a question, Ashley?"

"Yes," Ashley said with a shrug in my direction. "I asked why not."

It must have fit in with what Kastner was saying because he was immediately off explaining the mysteries of some abstraction that I was positive Ashley could have quoted verbatim from the textbook.

After class I caught up with Ashley. At six-teen, I didn't have to chase after girls. To tell the truth, they were usually following me around, but not Ashley. I don't think she ever followed anybody.

"What was all that about?" I asked. "I had a super new Swiftie for you and now I can't use it. Why did you do it? That isn't playing fair."

She looked at me as if I'd said something stupid. "I decided to go back to square one. I wanted to see what it felt like to flunk."

"Dumb!" I said, following her down the hall. "So how did it feel?"

"Wonderful!" she said, dodging through the General Math kids spilling from the classroom. "Human."

"I don't understand."

"Nobody understands me," she said, barely turning her head. "I bet you didn't know I used to pull the heads off my Barbie dolls, too."

"Why?" I caught up with her again.

"Because they were so maddeningly perfect."

"What did you do to Ken? Pull his head off too?" For some reason I wanted to keep her talking.

"No. I broke Ken's legs." Then she laughed and I knew she was putting me on.

"That's cheating, you know. Flunking on purpose." I sounded like Barbie's Ken.

"How do you figure?"

"Cheating to fail is as bad as cheating to win."

She stopped at her locker and shoved her trig

book up on the top shelf. "Tests make me feel like a laboratory rat. IQ, Achievement, Aptitude, Basic Skills, PSAT, ACT. Tests! Tests! And there'll be more, semester after semester, year after year until graduation or death, whichever comes first."

"I try not to think about it," I said.

"They must have my brain graphed in three dimensions. What they don't know yet is that there is a difference between a brain and a mind. The brain's a map. My mind's my own. At least they haven't figured out how to touch that."

Ordinarily Ashley looked like an elf, but when she got steamed up about something she became a miniature dervish, her eyes steely.

"Here in school they think everything is just as important as everything else," she went on, "but it isn't, is it?"

"I don't think so."

"There's got to be a reason for being, doesn't there?"

"Of course."

She slammed her locker door shut. "Why do they think, just because we have a brain, that we have to be challenged? What's so great about being smart? Why can't they let us live?"

"I guess they want us to live up to our potential." I sounded like Kastner.

"Potential!" she sneered. "Do you know what

potential is? The energy that a piece of matter has because of its position."

"Where'd you read that?"

"In a physics book Kastner gave me last week—to challenge me." She pretended to gag. "But, Joel. Flunking that test was fun. You should try it sometime. You'd be surprised how it makes you feel. Smug. You probably couldn't pull it off, though."

"I could too. If I wanted to."

"I'll believe it when I see it, Mr. Perfect." She touched my cheek lightly and ran down the hall.

※

It took me a good week to figure out how I was going to take Ashley up on her dare, and nearly two weeks to get ready. Mine wasn't going to be a spur-of-the-moment thing like flunking Kastner's measly test. Mine would be carefully planned and thought out.

Miss Jacobs's idea of Advanced English was quantity. We had a required reading list and every Friday we had to hand in a critical analysis of one of the books we had read that week. Ashley usually read three. I managed one.

Just before class that Monday, I waited for Ashley out in the hall.

"You know what?" I grinned at her. "I'm going

to find out what it feels like to be human today."

"You mean you didn't turn in your analysis last Friday?" Ashley fell back against the wall as if she were going to faint.

"No," I went on. "I handed one in—a critical analysis on a book that doesn't even exist. *The Point of Every Return* by Isaac Kucinski. I made it up. Plot, characters, theme, the works. I said it was a little-known translation from the Polish that my mom had picked up for me."

"You didn't!" Ashley squeaked between giggles.

I didn't know if this was what it felt like to be human, but it certainly was beginning to feel like fun.

"You see, I copied down all the big words I could find in the *New York Times Book Review* section, quoted reviews, those who gave it a good review and one that panned it. I spent hours on it. Don't say I can't take a dare, so here goes," and I walked into class.

Everybody's paper was graded and lying on the corner of each desk, except mine.

"How is it feeling to be human?" Ashley whispered.

I winked back at her and waited to be told off but good by Miss Jacobs, who stood up, stepped in front of her desk, looked around the class, and coughed softly. She was holding my paper!

"Class," she began, "I was most pleased with your papers this week, but I was particularly pleased with one. As I have always told you, a class like this must never settle for the mediocre. You must take the initiative to strike out on your own. You must use your talents to the utmost and today I wish to read to you an example of just that type of talent and initiative."

I scrunched down in my seat. She believed it was for real! I didn't dare look over at Ashley. Jacobs began to read. I couldn't stand it. I looked out the window. The city stretched out as far as I could see, so flat you could almost see into tomorrow. Miss Jacobs read on and on. I began to believe she could read a Sears catalogue and make it "meaningful." That was her favorite word. "Think meaningful thoughts. Write meaningful ideas. Read meaningful works."

I could see Ashley and her reaction without even turning my head. I knew just how she was looking. She'd have that intense look blanketing her face as if she were absorbing every "meaningful" idea, her chin tilted up, her pencil poised to jot down a pertinent point, but underneath she'd be gloating hysterically at how I'd flunked flunking or failed failing or whatever.

"As you can readily see," Miss Jacobs folded my paper and laid it on my desk, "this certainly deserves the highest of grades. You know I seldom give an *A* and never an *A* +, but this analysis richly deserves that rating. Thank you, Joel, for this perceptive analysis."

I looked up at her finally and nodded, accepting my well-undeserved praise. As for Ashley, I tried to pretend she wasn't sitting across the aisle from me, but Ashley was never one I could pretend wasn't there.

And, of course, she *was* always there, so much a natural part of my life that I didn't think about her any more than I thought about where I lived or the church we sometimes attended or what college I'd eventually go to. It wasn't that I didn't care; it was just something I never had to worry about. That's probably why I never asked her for a date—a real date. We always ended up in the same places anyway.

"Who are you taking to the game tonight?"

"Karen. Who are you going with?"

"Martin."

"Why Martin?"

"Why not?"

"See you there."

Though we certainly never talked about it because there was no reason to bother, we both figured that sooner or later, sometime in the far future after we'd done the college routine and gotten into the serious business of living, we'd just sort of naturally spend the rest of our lives together.

If I could go back and do and say things differently, I would. Maybe that's why history is so hard to believe. You know the way it turns out, but it's impossible to put the pieces together again to see *how* it happened. It's like knowing the answer to a math problem, but not understanding *how* you know.

And that year I didn't understand why—on top of all the time she spent with her horse—Ashley was suddenly writing a weekly column for the school newspaper without telling me. Somehow it didn't seem fair just to pick up a copy of the *Bradgate Badger* and find Ashley's name under something called *Willie-Waught*. She could have at least told me what she was going to do.

All the kids were standing around in the halls before school reading her column when I spotted Ashley.

"So you're aiming for the Pulitzer," I said, tapping her on the shoulder with my rolled-up newspaper. "But what's this *Willie-Waught*? You made it up didn't you?"

"Of course not! Webster did. Go look it up for yourself."

"What does it mean?" I was lazy when it came to checking words in a dictionary. To tell the truth, I usually asked Ashley.

"It means a cheering sip—or quaff—or draught. Whatever. Don't you like it?"

"Sure. But nobody knows what it means."

"It can be a learning experience then, probably one of the few they'll get here at Badgerville. Rah rah."

"So, Ashley the intellectual cheerleader, helping us cope with the ills of our world."

Ashley stopped in the middle of the hall traffic and faked a kick at my shin. "No! It's going to be funny. I'm going to point out how ridiculous life is. How we're living in an age of absurdity. And then, just for kicks, I'm going to slip in a new word every week. A word no one knows the meaning of."

"Show-off," I kidded her. "You mean you're going to improve your readers' vocabularies?"

"No! That's the fun. I'm going to make up the word. A different word every week and see how long it takes someone to catch on."

I helped her make up words for her column. We made up *knarfish, bibuless, acathon, gafferite.* Ashley was called on that last one, but she said it meant to correct an error and everyone believed her.

I kept her last column. I don't know why. Maybe I just neglected to throw it away.

```
WILLIE-WAUGHT

by

I. WANDA NO
```

We are starting a Be-an-Individual Week here at Bradgate High. For just one week out of the year, everyone is to sit around and be a complete individual. Just think, for fifty-one weeks we can be ourselves.

———————

A rolling stone gathers no moss, but who likes moss? All that glitters is as good as gold. If silence is golden, we've lost a fortune. I know a lot of old idioms—by old idiots!

———————

French Lesson:
carte blanche—take Blanche home.
coup de grace—cut the grass.
au contraire—away from the city.
à la carte—on the wagon.

———————

I would like to know a person of mystery. The people I know are interesting, attractive, and amusing, but not even a little mysterious. Many years of my brevite life have been spent looking for such a person. At various times I have noticed dark, ominous-looking persons with furtive ways and slouch hats. Aha, I've thought, here is a P.O.M. (Person of Mystery). But when I get to know them, they are always something everyday-like. I mean with jobs like grocery-sackers or sump-pumpers. By the time I've found that out, they're my friends and I can't very well say, "You're very nice, but you're not a Person of Mystery, so I guess I can't bother with you anymore."

———————

I am not really conceited, not when you get to know me—just ask my only friend.

———————

Vocabulary Lesson:

Gnu—as in "No gnus is good gnus."

Cadillac—as in "A cad-ill-ac mean if you
  pull its tail."

Custard—as in "Custard's Last Stand."

Today I glanced through my window
into the garden and saw a duckbill platypus at rest in my shoe tree. The first
platypus of autumn had come and my little heart expanded with joy. I leaped
on my Pogo stick and sought the quiet of
the countryside. Let others have the
wondrous ocean, rugged mountains,
or green forests—I'll take 160 acres of
Iowa farmland—or what it's worth
in cash.

The Bradgate seniors tried to find a
good class motto last week. Here are some
of the ones suggested. They were not se-
lected, however.

Face life squarely, and you'll get it square
  in the face.

Don't be a cigarette and make an ash of
  yourself.

It's not what you send (cash, check, or
  money order). It's how much you send.

Yesterday is gone; tomorrow may never come. And who cares?

I can go no farther. My water has given out and there is only one dry crust of bread left in my knapsack. i hardly have the strength to hold down the shift key. i face the burning desert on one hand, and a band of murderous bedouins on the other. So, good-bye forever!

One day, it must have been the beginning of our junior year because the sun was warm, the sky blue-washed, and the leaves on the oaks and maples in front of school such a splash of color that after I parked the car, I leaned against the hood and wondered why kids had to be locked up in classrooms on such a day. I was beginning to think Ashley's Beatlemania was catching because I started humming "It's Getting Better All the Time." But then Ashley herself came dashing across the parking lot. "Did Ann Kelsey call you? About Homecoming King?"

"Sure. Why?"

"You aren't going to nominate Kenny, are you?"

"Why not? I think it's sort of funny, don't you?"

Ashley put her backpack down on the sidewalk and moved closer. She smelled wonderful, but she always smelled wonderful no matter how much time she spent at the stables with her new horse Life Line. She said that was the one advantage of money; it could buy expensive perfume. Ashley didn't care about clothes; in fact, her mother picked them out for her and tried to make sure Ashley wore them in the right combination. But sometime in the process of our growing up she had developed a passion for perfume. Never too much, of course, but just enough to make me want to close my eyes and inhale her.

"If you nominate him, I'll . . . I'll . . ." Evidently she couldn't think of anything bad enough to threaten me with so she just stood there glaring up at me. That probably made her even madder. She was barely five feet tall and I was six feet one then and hoping I wouldn't keep on growing.

"It's not nice, and he can't help it," Ashley went on, "if he's in love with computers and has that white skin and . . ."

"And," I added just to tease her, "bright red hair which he inherited from his white-faced, red-haired parent. He probably can't even answer the phone without blushing."

It was a lot worse than blushing. Kenny didn't turn sort of pink the way most people did. He managed high-tech, state-of-the-art, living color whenever anyone as much as noticed him. If anyone ever wanted to keep a low profile, to sort of melt into the woodwork, it was Kenny. He even cringed when teachers called his name in class. He wasn't shy. He was paranoid about people looking at him.

I guess that's why the TAGS were always nominating him for every office or honor. First it was class president, the president of Honor Society, and now this—Homecoming King. In junior high, we'd nicknamed him Flag until his parents complained to the principal. Except for his blue eyes, he had only two colors: white and red. As a television set, he'd have been worth a million.

"It's Ann Kelsey's idea of fun to nominate him. It's cruel—like catching a firefly and putting it in a jar." She stopped, took a deep breath, and began again. "She wants us TAGS to vote as a bloc because some guys from the football team will be nominated and Ann figures their votes will be split, and poor Kenny will win and have to go to the stupid Homecoming Dance and spend the whole evening with his face matching his hair." She took another gulp of air. "And worst of all, he'll need a date. You know he'll die if he has to ask a girl. . . . I think the whole thing stinks!"

She bent down to pick up her backpack. I bent down and sniffed her hair.

"You, on the other hand, smell like a steamed kumquat. What do you want me to do?"

"Oh, go ahead and nominate him as long as you told Ann you would, but I'm going to nominate someone else."

"Who?"

"Mr. Perfect." She pretended to brush some lint from my sweater.

"You wouldn't dare!"

"Watch me. That way the TAG vote will be split too."

There wasn't much more either of us could say, so we walked into school only about five minutes late for homeroom. We didn't have to worry much about being tardy; after all, we were the top of the TAGS.

Ashley's idea, plausible as it was, didn't work. Kenny flamed as Homecoming King, flanked by two football players as attendants. I was runner-up King, which sounded as stupid as I felt crowning Candi, the cheerleader, the new Homecoming Queen. It was Kenny's duty to give her the traditional kiss on the cheek. I almost felt sorry for him at that point.

Kenny had a date that night, though—Ashley. I danced with her once and tried to find out who had asked whom. She smiled, a bit too sweetly, patted my arm, and said, quoting her Beatles again, "Let it be."

I never did find out the truth.

The rest of that semester we were so busy that we had no time to live, leisure to dream, or space to think. Things happened of which we were part, but few of them were important. Bradgate High calendared us, week after week, in neat little squares of dates: basketball, swimming meets, school plays, speech contests, music festivals, and tests. We were prodded to learn, learn, learn as if the world would collapse if our PSAT scores dipped a point from the school's proud, highest-in-the-state average.

I gave Ashley a ride home from school one cold November day before Thanksgiving. We had taken an afternoon's worth of tests on our Higher Level Thinking Skills.

"Do you suppose people in the Alps do better on Higher Level Thinking than people who live at sea level?" Ashley curled up in the front seat beside me.

"I wouldn't know. Maybe they'll test us next on our Lower Level Thinking Skills."

"Never," Ashley answered. "That would be too basic."

She waited for me to groan at the bad pun. Instead, I pulled out onto the freeway which both of us hated, but which was faster than taking the side streets. Besides, I knew that the Christmas decorations that were already up in front of houses would drive Ashley bonkers. I didn't like them either, not before Thanksgiving.

"How did you answer that question about what would have happened if Custer had won at Little Big Horn? The only thing I could think of was that Custer's Last Stand—that country western bar over on Third Street—would have to come up with a different name."

"It was a stupid, iffy question." Ashley punched the seat. "You can't change things that have already happened. There's no way to go backward and make things different. Besides, Custer is probably one of my least favorite people in American history."

"Yes, I know. But how did you answer it?"

"I said they changed the state's name from Montana to Custer. Custer ran for President, won, and shipped all the Native Americans down to Panama, where they were used as slave labor to dig the canal."

"How depressing," I said, intending a Swiftie. I managed an exit from the freeway. The houses were bigger, the lawns more expansive as we drew closer to home.

"All that Higher Level Thinking must have cut off the oxygen supply to your brain. I think that's the effect holidays have on me."

"I thought you liked Thanksgiving," I said as the white stones in the drive crunched under the tires.

"Thanksgiving is possible," she admitted, "if you're not a turkey. But Christmas . . ." Ashley scowled at me as if it were my fault. "What a commercial thing to do to a perfectly nice little baby."

"You don't mean that," I said, knowing very well that she probably did. "You're just trying to dream up something outrageous for your column."

"What a wonderful idea." She gave me one of her most angelic smiles. "Maybe I'll dedicate it to you." She got out of the car and stood by the open door. "I'll work on it tonight and show it to you tomorrow."

I didn't bother to answer. I just waved at her back as she disappeared into the house.

Ashley didn't get a chance to show anything to me the next day because I ran into Triss instead. Literally ran into her, I mean. I was supposed to meet a buddy for racquetball across town and I was late and in a hurry, so I was half running down the hall toward the front door. I rounded the corner and sent someone sailing into a perfect pratfall.

The first thing I noticed was her coat. You have to understand about coats at Bradgate. No matter what the season of the year only two kinds of students spent all day covered up: the real losers who must have felt that they were wearing some kind of armor against the world and the drama freaks. Sometimes it was a little hard to tell the difference, but not with Triss.

She was wearing a long black coat with a velvet collar and no buttons. It was something my great-grandfather might have worn to the opera. On her, it looked great.

I must have looked like an idiot. She leaned back on both elbows and said, "Do you always stand around with your mouth open?"

"Not really," I managed.

Somewhere in the far corner of my mind, a little alarm signal went off, warning, "Nope! No way! Don't do it! Mistake!" I ignored the alarm.

"After we go to the hospital, if they don't keep you, will you go out to dinner with me?" I took both her hands and helped her up. "My name's Joel and I'm really a very nice person. I can even supply references."

"Don't you ever watch where you're going?" She made several swipes at the dust clinging to her coat.

"Not anymore," I said, taking her arm and steering her toward the hall door.

She *was* beautiful! That doesn't happen very often, seeing someone in real life who is 100 percent, full-time, certifiably gorgeous: shoulder-length black hair with the blackest of eyes, which when she stood up were almost on a level with mine.

"Where did you come from?" I asked as we walked out to my car.

"Drama class." She didn't just walk like an ordinary person; she floated.

"I mean before that." Bradgate was a big school, but I could never not have seen her. "What grade are you in?"

"I'm a senior. I just came here last week. I'm living with my aunt. I'll be here till June." Her voice was as lovely as she was.

I ignored the "until June" part. That was months away and I didn't want to think of losing something I'd just discovered. "So if you just got here last week, it's my duty on behalf of Bradgate High to acquaint you with the wonders of our city." I held the car door open for her.

"Wow! Where'd you get a car like this?" She settled back into the seat.

I missed my game of racquetball that afternoon and what would have been a fifteen-minute drive to take Triss home turned into two hours. We began with Logan Park and the Science Museum, and we never stopped talking, at least I didn't. Somehow it seemed important to me that we catch up on all the time we'd not known each other. We were half-

way through seventh grade when I looked at my
watch. It was nearly six and I was starving. I didn't
think Triss would do anything as mundane as eat,
but I said, "Look, there's a place near here called
Jimmy's. They have great *fajitas*."

"I'll have to call home. I don't want my aunt
calling the police."

I didn't know how such ordinary words like "I'll
have to call home" could sound like poetry, but
they did.

I chose Jimmy's for two reasons. The food was
good and, two, I was pretty sure that at six o'clock
we wouldn't run into anyone from Bradgate. I
wasn't in the mood to share. But when we walked
into the restaurant, people I'd never seen before
turned and looked and smiled. At first I thought
they were probably some of Dad's friends who had
seen me around the club, but then I decided I wasn't
the one they were smiling at. It was Triss, and she
was smiling back.

I ate without tasting. I talked without thinking,
I watched without staring. By the time we finished
eating, we were up to our first year in high school.
Nothing about us matched: where we lived or how
we lived or what we'd done, but everything fit as
neatly and as snugly as pieces of a jigsaw puzzle.
By the time we walked back to the car I was floating
too. I didn't know whether Triss was feeling the

same way I was, but for the moment it didn't matter.

Triss's aunt, I soon discovered, lived only a dozen or two blocks from our house. The streets that had been familiar to me all my life became suddenly important, as if I were seeing them for the first time.

I walked with her through the early darkness to the front door. She turned to me, and with one hand as light as the brush of a butterfly's wing, she touched my cheek. "You know, JoJo, that was a terrific dinner. I think the rest of this school year is going to be just great. Don't you?"

I did indeed. As I drove home, a song from one of Ashley's Beatles albums kept running over and over through my mind: "Something in the way she moves . . ." The song had never been one of Ashley's favorites.

"Who won?" Mom asked as I wandered into the living room. She was curled up in a chair by the fireplace with a glass of sherry, a note pad, and her address book. "It must have been you. You're wearing a rather triumphant smile."

I had completely forgetten the racquetball game. I'd have to call and apologize.

"I didn't play. I fell in love instead."

"That's nice," Mom said still concentrating on her list. Then her head came up as if she'd received an electric shock. "You what?"

"Love," I said. "*L-O-V-E* with an exclamation point."

"I thought that's what you said. Have you eaten? Your father won't be home for dinner, and I'm going out, so you'd better tell Esther if you want her to fix you something."

I sprawled on the couch across from her. "I've just told you the single most important fact of my life and you ask me if I've eaten."

She put down her pen and picked up her sherry. "It's your father's fault. Nutrition first. Emotion later."

I knew she was teasing me and it usually worked. I remembered how I used to come in from playing with the neighbor kids, crying because someone had hurt me. "Is it bleeding?" she'd ask. If I said no, she'd say, "If it's not bleeding, it doesn't hurt."

"So you finally really looked at Ashley." She smiled at me.

"Her name is Triss," I began. Ten minutes later I was still talking, until the phone rang and interrupted me.

When Mom came back, she stood in the doorway. "I wonder who her parents are."

"I don't know. I just met her today. She's living with her aunt in a condo over on Fifth. And her father's an executive for some computer company."

"Well, darling, it all sounds perfectly wonderful.

I'm sure she's a delightful girl. I must go now. You get a good night's sleep." She rubbed the top of my head, the way she used to do when I was a kid. "Perhaps you'll feel all better in the morning."

The next morning when I came down for breakfast, Dad didn't say anything but just reached out and grabbed my wrist.

"What are you doing?" I asked.

"Checking your pulse. Your mother says you may have come down with a virulent disease common to your age group and sex."

I looked over at Mom, who was hiding behind the morning paper. "Love, exclamation point," she said. "Why else would you be up at this hour on a Saturday?"

"What happened to Ashley?" Dad asked as if I were one of his patients.

"Nothing ever happens to Ashley. She happens to the world." I poured myself a glass of milk. "I, on the other hand, have been happened to. This is a crazy question, but have either of you ever been in love? I mean really in love."

They didn't take me very seriously that morning, but when I brought Triss to dinner the next week they began to believe me.

If I hadn't already known that Triss was honest-to-god 100 percent beautiful, one look at my parents' faces would have convinced me. Of course, they didn't exactly stare at her, but Dad, looking as if I'd walked in with the crown jewels or whatever the American equivalent is, almost overdid his courtly father-host act. Mom, on the other hand, looked as if she were seeing something straight out of *Star Trek*. Maybe it was Triss's outfit. I had to admit it was a bit theatrical for Mom, who always preached "less is more" when it came to clothes. I hoped Triss hadn't noticed Mom's reaction.

Later came the after-dinner coffee and the inevitable questions about Triss's family—inevitable, in part because Triss wasn't one of the usual blue-eyed blondes who filled the halls of Bradgate High and made up half the population of the city in which we lived. She also didn't have two sets of grandparents who had known *my* grandparents.

It was Dad, not Mom, who made the first move. He usually left the social stuff for her to do since he had a habit of making the most casual question sound as if he were inquiring about the symptoms of some terminal disease.

"And your parents," he began. "Joel tells us your father is with a computer outfit and you're just here until June?" At least he made it sound like a question instead of a diagnosis.

"Dad's based in San Diego, but he calls himself a 'fixer.' Whenever there's a problem in the company, he spends however long it takes, wherever it is, to try and make things better. It's sort of like you, I suppose. I mean, he's kind of a company doctor."

Dad ate it up. He's the highest-priced surgeon in town, but he likes to think of himself as your basic good old general practitioner.

Mom took over. "Joel's father's work seldom takes him farther than an operating room. But how did you end up here?"

I wasn't sure whether she meant in our city or in our house.

"Mom and Dad are hopscotching from Bangkok to Taiwan to Hong Kong to Dallas. I'm staying with my aunt. But it's hard to come into a new school, especially one as prestigious as Bradgate. Joel's been wonderful." She smiled at me and I was glad that I was sitting down. "Of course, I miss the beach and all the kids at the club. . . ." Her voice trailed off as she stared down at her coffee cup.

"You know, it just occurs to me," Dad began, obviously touched by the emotion in her voice. "Perhaps I could arrange to get you a guest card from *our* club. A junior guest card, that is. Joel and his friend Ashley and a lot of the other kids from Bradgate practically grew up there."

This time it was Dad who got the full benefit of Triss's dazzling smile. "Oh, Doctor Logan, that's really kind of you. But are you sure it wouldn't be too much trouble?"

Before Dad could answer, Mom said, "You better check first. There may not be any junior cards left." She turned to Triss. "It's just a silly thing about numbers, you know."

It had never occurred to me that Triss would miss anything as simple as belonging to the club. For Ashley and me, it had always seemed like some kind of obligation to pacify our parents. I could have kicked myself for not having thought of the guest card before Dad did. On the other hand, it wasn't going to make any difference. Triss was going to be my personal, escorted guest from then on.

I finally took Triss home, and as I walked her to the door, she said, "I'm glad to have met your parents, Joel. They're very nice, but don't be surprised if the quota on guest cards is full."

"It won't be."

"Want to bet? Your mother didn't like me."

"Don't be silly."

"No really. I could tell. She watched every move I made, and I'm positive she memorized every word I said."

I really wasn't interested in discussing my mother at that point. I kissed Triss instead, for the first time, and for a long time.

I would have lost the bet. When I got home, Mom and Dad were sitting in the library waiting for me.

"She's a lovely girl, Joel," Dad began, "and as charming as she is attractive."

"She's certainly extremely mature," Mom said. "It's hard to believe she's still in high school. But perhaps young women grow up faster in Southern California than they do here. What is it they call it? Life in the fast lane?"

"Then I'll just have to shift gears, won't I?" I sat down on the edge of the couch. "But, seriously, isn't she fantastic? And she really liked you a lot. She said so."

"Listen, son," Dad said, looking uncomfortable. "Your mother and I are a little embarrassed."

Mom laughed and patted Dad's leg. "We should have checked first. Your father called Bud Kingsley and, wouldn't you know, just our luck. All the junior guest cards have been taken for the next six months. I mean your father actually pleaded with him, but you know how it is. If he made one exception . . ."

"Maybe you can explain to Triss." Dad fidgeted with his coffee cup.

"No need," I said slowly. "Triss had a feeling that there might be a problem."

"Oh, problem's not the word. It's red tape. The

numbers and rules, you know." Mom sounded a little like a speeded-up recording.

"No big deal," I said getting up. "She won't be missing a thing. She can be my guest. I've already asked her to go with me to the New Year's dance at the club."

"But what about Ashley?" Mom asked.

I shrugged. "What about her? She'll be there too. She always is."

Before I went to bed that night, I listened to one of the Beatles records Ashley had given me. I fell asleep somewhere in the middle of "Lovely Rita, Meter Maid," thinking that there was no problem even though the quotas were filled. Triss was beyond quotas.

※

It was the next to the last school day before Christmas vacation when I remembered that I'd not only shrugged Ashley off, I'd forgotten her. Not really forgotten her. That would have been impossible. Bradgate High allowed only five minutes between classes, so there was never any time to talk very long in the hall, and because juniors and seniors had open campus at lunch, most days Triss and I spent at the sandwich shop up the street.

What I'd really forgotten was a kind of ritual or habit, maybe, that Ashley and I had shared ever since seventh grade. That year we were trying to figure out something to get for our parents' Christmas presents. There was nothing they needed and nothing that they particularly wanted as far as we could think until Ashley came up with one of her better ideas.

"I've got it!" She grabbed my arm on the way out of school that day.

"Got what?" I asked, following her. I had to follow her since she still was holding on to my arm with both hands. "The Bradgate Plague?" Half the kids in school had been home with some kind of virus and I wasn't enthusiastic about catching it just in time for the holidays. Besides Mom and Dad and I were planning on a neat trip to St. Thomas and I didn't want to miss it.

"The perfect place to find the acceptable present for the parents."

"I thought you were going to enroll them in Save the Snails."

Ashley looked serious for a minute. "You mean they're in danger too?" She let go of my sleeve and punched me in the shoulder. "You shouldn't make jokes about serious things."

"I didn't know snails were serious things. Anyway, where are we going?"

She stopped walking and pointed.

"You mean the Art Center?"

"The gift shop. They have lots of neat things, but there are some really tacky things too, paintings and ceramics and whatnot. All we have to do is pick out the very worst, assure our parents they came from some struggling artists, and we've made everybody feel good."

"Everybody?" We pushed through the big front doors.

"Sure. The artists because they'd probably never sell whatever it is to anyone else. Our parents because they can feel they're building our esthetic sensibility, and us because . . . it'll be fun, won't it? Doing something together and different from everyone else."

That's how our crazy Christmas shopping sprees began and we'd done it ever since and that's what I'd almost forgotten this Triss Christmas. I caught up with Ashley just before English class and reminded her that the next afternoon should be our annual outing to the Art Center. She looked at me as if I had told her something so obvious that it didn't need saying. It occurred to me then that Ashley was perfectly capable of having totally ignored what half the kids in school knew—that Triss and I were a pair.

She smiled, much too sweetly for Ashley, and said, "I thought you were going to plead temporary insanity."

"What are you talking about?" I tried to act innocent.

"Love. Exclamation point."

I wondered if she'd been talking to Mom.

"I'm not blind, you know."

"So?" I waited to see if I cared what she said.

"Maybe you're growing up." I wasn't sure she really meant it. "And you're getting ready to ask if Triss can go along with us? Right?"

"Right. Do you mind?" It was a stupid question. Ashley would never do anything she didn't want to do.

Still I felt better when she said, "Not really."

By the time Triss and I got to the Art Center the next day, Ashley was already there, sitting on the steps waiting for us.

"Hi, Triss," she greeted us. I didn't really expect her to say hi to me because I guess as far as Ashley and I were concerned, we were givens, and givens didn't need to be acknowledged. I held the door open and Ashley and Triss went in. "If you've never been here before," Ashley guided Triss down the hall, "you must see . . ."

I followed, beginning to feel like the third party who turns a company into a crowd, but that didn't last long because, as always, Ashley had an unerring eye for the most exciting works. I'd been through the place at least four times with our Honors Art class and listened to so many hours of "esthetic critiques" that I thought nothing could surprise me. Ashley did. She picked out all my favorites to show Triss.

We stopped under a Calder mobile. "It's an early Calder," Ashley explained. "Isn't it amazing? To think he thought up the idea of making art out of mobiles."

Triss glanced at the mobile. "You sure it isn't a joke?"

Ashley looked at me, her face frozen into a placid smile.

We walked around the Rodin sculpture of Balzac. "Gross," Triss commented.

Ashley grinned. "Well, earthy, at least." This time Ashley did not look at me. We stopped in front of a Mondrian, its perfect squares, rectangles, and lines aglow with contrast.

"Something so clean and precise about it," Ashley murmured.

Triss tilted her head from one side to the other. "It'd make great colors for a stage set."

This time Ashley turned to me. "Are you still with us, Joel?"

I refused to answer. I stayed and pretended to be studying the Mondrian.

By the time we'd covered three of the main galleries of paintings, statues, and mobiles, I decided to call a halt. "And this way to the gift shop," I said. Triss might be a super actress, but the other arts were definitely not her bag. There was nothing wrong with that, of course, but I didn't want to think she was less than perfect.

I'd already explained the point of Ashley's and my presents-for-parents game to Triss. She hadn't quite understood why we thought it was funny enough to do every year, but once inside the shop, we took off in three different directions looking for possible atrocities. It wasn't difficult. There were a lot of really nice things, of course, because some very talented artists from all over the country had their works on display there. The best bets for ultimate tackiness were on the ceramic shelves, but Ashley had beat me to them. That was another one of our unspoken rules—we couldn't buy the same things.

I was trying to make a final choice between a wood carving that looked like a cross between a water buffalo and a Shetland pony and a watercolor of a sunset that should have been titled "Upset Stomach" when I looked up and saw Triss motioning to me.

"It isn't tacky," she said, "but do look at this. Isn't it lovely?"

I took the kaleidoscope from her. It wasn't brass

like the one I'd broken when I was a kid; instead it was made of some rich, dark, polished wood. When I held it up to the light and turned it, the colors inside glowed as if they were alive and dropped into patterns of Mondrian perfection.

"Oh, Joel. Your parents will love it. Really love it, I mean. They ought to. Look how much it costs."

"I don't know, Triss. It isn't . . . it really isn't quite what I had in mind."

"You can tell your parents I helped choose it."

I didn't have any choice. I took the kaleidoscope up to the cash register. Ashley looked down at it, then up at me, and burst out laughing.

"What's so funny?" Triss floated up beside me.

"I don't know," I said trying to stare Ashley down. "This present, I guess."

"Oh, Ashley. Don't you know what it is?" Triss picked up our gift. "See. You look through here and turn and . . ."

"And all the little pieces fall into place. Isn't that clever of them?" Ashley smiled her little sweet smile and placed her gift on the counter. It was something that must have been meant as a soup tureen because it came complete with a clumsy clay ladle and a cover that looked vaguely like a cabbage left too long in the refrigerator.

"It's certainly different," Triss said, removing the cover and looking inside. "What made you decide on this?"

"There's something so blatant about it." Ashley smiled over at me. "And it matches exactly the way Joel's brain works most of the time."

I tried to think of a suitably insulting reply, but Ashley, with another of her inane smiles, waved one hand and walked out of the gift shop.

As Triss and I headed for my car, she squeezed my hand. "Ashley is so sweet, isn't she?"

I wondered if Triss's comment was as phony as Ashley's smiles.

I never understood the effect New Year's Eve had on people, including my parents, who were relatively sensible and usually didn't take the social stuff too seriously. I wondered if once a year they had to remind themselves that all the money and all those stocks and bonds and companies and those buildings with the family's names really *did* belong to them. The rest of the time they joked about how everything belonged to their lawyers.

On New Year's Eve when I was a little kid, they'd get the baby-sitter for me and let me stay up an hour later than usual. That was fine because it gave me time to finish a book I was reading and

I didn't have to worry about one of them coming in and flipping off my bedside light just in the middle of an exciting sentence.

When they decided I was old enough not to ruin my health by staying up until midnight, they started hauling me along to the club with them. Without Ashley it would have been boring. As it was, we spent the evening with a bunch of kids we'd known forever and watched television or played video games or laughed at the adults until it was time for our parents to round us up and take us home. Ashley insisted it was a kind of sneaky training session to insure that we'd act the same way as they did when we grew up.

This year Triss and I got to the club a bit late, but early enough to meet Ashley and her parents. I introduced Triss and they went through the little hum of conversation and smiling exclamations and nods that people are supposed to do with introductions. We headed for our table, the parents like an advance guard, Triss and Ashley and I bringing up the rear as if I was supposed to fend off attackers.

The place was New Year's Eve noisy—all very polite, of course, but several decibels louder than a normal evening. The band, a very good one really, had already begun the night's worth of sixties and seventies music that usually ended with a medley of Beatles songs.

Dad and Ashley's father were busy pulling out chairs for our mothers, and I did the same for Triss and Ashley, except that when I got to Ashley there was just one chair left. The table had been set for six. Ashley caught it at the same time as I did and said, just loudly enough for our parents to hear, "How quaint! They must have thought we'd like to play musical chairs. When the music stops, Joel, I'll race you for the seat."

It was evident she was ticked off about something, but I couldn't quite understand what. On a night as busy as this it would be easy for the staff to foul things up. Dad and Saunders, Ashley's father, made a major production signalling a bus boy and getting another chair and table setting. After what seemed like half an hour, but was really only a few minutes, I was seated between Ashley and Triss. It was Ashley's mother who turned nothing into a disaster, rating somewhere between the sinking of the *Titanic* and the beginning of World War III.

She began with "Oh, my dear" to the table at large and then to Triss in particular, "I'm so used to just the six of us on New Year's Eve. Oh. Triss. It is Triss, isn't it? It's not that you're an outsider and that this is a closed party, but . . ."

Old Smoothy Saunders came to her rescue. "It was my fault. Ashley told me seven and I forgot."

Then Mom and Dad got into the act. "It's perfectly all right, Celia," Mom said. "Everyone has a place now. We are seven. Don't you remember that little poem by Longfellow? Or was it Wordsworth? We had to memorize it in school. I don't remember how it begins, but I know how it ends:

> *"Twas throwing words away, for still*
> *The little maid would have her will,*
> *And said, 'Nay, we are seven!' "*

Dad and Saunders applauded, Celia leaned over and patted Mom's hand, and I thought Mom was going to give an encore, but fortunately the waiter came for drink orders.

Ashley leaned over to me. "We are seven. They've finally learned to count."

It wasn't the greatest beginning for an evening and it didn't get a whole lot better, except for the times I danced with Triss. The parents ended up sitting at other people's tables as they did every year, which was fine, but it was Ashley who took the edge off any possible fun.

We'd been talking about Bradgate High and how great it was that the semester had finally ended.

"I'm not going back next semester," Ashley announced with as much expression as a grocery clerk's "Have a nice day," but I knew she was waiting gleefully for my reaction.

Triss was watching the dance floor, where the older generation were attempting to jitterbug to a very loud and fast "Tuxedo Junction," and didn't hear Ashley's pronouncement.

"What do you mean?" I practically growled at her.

"I'm going to be a page. At the State Legislature. Dad thought it would look good on my college application, and I thought how wonderful to drop out of it all for a semester."

"A page? Will the legislators provide you with a little red, white, and blue tunic so you can run around in your slippers with turned up toes? How about a lute? Will they provide that too?"

"You're just jealous. While I'm helping turn the wheels of state government, you'll be locked in calculus and American Ideas and all those meaningful things."

I wasn't jealous, of course, and I'd probably be so busy that I wouldn't even miss her, but that wasn't the point. I sat there trying to figure out what exactly was the point.

"What does a page do?" Triss asked after Ashley explained what we'd been talking about. "Won't it put you a semester behind in school?"

"Ashley probably has enough credits to graduate now," I said. "She just hangs around Bradgate so she won't have to face the real world."

Ashley ignored me. "A page is a kind of gofer. Mostly they run errands for the legislators, but it is a chance to see how state government really works, and there are some important bills coming up this session."

"Like save the mayflies?" I suggested.

They both ignored me.

"I think it sounds great," Triss said. "You'll meet a lot of important people and you'll be doing something that matters—that's real."

"But what you'll be doing is real, too," Ashley said. "You're new here, but getting the lead in the spring musical at Bradgate ranks right up there with receiving an Academy Award as far as this town is concerned."

"It can't hurt," Triss agreed. "I can use all the exposure I can get. Besides, I need the experience. I have so much to learn."

"If you want to learn about acting, you should see Ashley at a horse show," I said, determined to get back in the conversation.

"Horse show?" Triss looked at Ashley.

"See, the season ends in August with the big horse show at the fairgrounds, and every year since she was big enough to fit into a saddle, Ashley's been there hauling in blue ribbons and silver cups. She rides every day of the week, you know."

"What's riding got to do with acting?" Triss looked puzzled.

"Because she hates the phoniness of the show ring."

"Joel's just being nasty." Ashley leaned both elbows on the table. "He's actually afraid of horses. You should have seen him the last time he rode. It was a jumping class and he fell off twice and his horse refused jumps three times."

"Wouldn't that disqualify him?" I hoped Triss was concerned.

"Sure," Ashley went on. "But since the prize was the Logan Cup, they let him make another round after the cup was awarded. His grandfather donated the cup years ago when the society horse show was just started."

"*Let* me?" I almost shouted. "They *made* me get back on that animal. But I got through all the jumps, didn't I?"

Ashley started to laugh. "Yes, and then you threw up on the way out of the ring." She stopped, her voice serious. "It *was* a rotten thing to do to a kid, wasn't it? He was only ten," she explained to Triss.

Then Ashley and I started trading stories about

the whole horse-show routine—the horse-show mothers, the politics, the crazy trainers, and the whole ridiculous world that Ashley was still a part of. The more Triss laughed, the more we exaggerated, and for a little while I forgot that I was ticked at Ashley.

Things were just beginning to get better when George Stratford sauntered over to our table. With him was a big, good-looking guy that George introduced to us as Mel somebody. Mel was a grinner and he had a lot of very white teeth to grin with. He grinned at me. He grinned at Triss, and he not only grinned at Ashley, he pulled out a chair, straddled it backward, his hands resting on the back, and said to only Ashley, "George tells me you're going to be a page, Ashley."

I didn't like the way he said Ashley. He sort of rolled it around with his tongue before he pronounced it. I turned to Triss, but George was standing beside her, his hand resting casually on her shoulder. "Would you care to dance, Triss? I think we're due for a slower number any minute, and when it comes to dancing, I'm a slow-numbers man."

Triss looked at me. The gentleman I was, I nodded and smiled. As they left, I turned toward Ashley, but she and the Grinner were leaving for the dance floor too, and there I sat alone at the vacant table, feeling like a glass of flat champagne. To make things worse, when the dance number was over, Ashley and the Grinner sat down on one side of me and Triss and George sat down on the other side, and for the rest of the evening we were *five*!

George had just graduated midyear from college, and he was filling Triss in on all his plans for a career in television; and from what I could overhear of Ashley and the Grinner, I learned that he was a junior in college, a frat brother of "good old George," and that if things worked out right he himself might land a part-time job with a lobbyist for the duration of the state legislature.

I finally excused myself and went to the men's room. I was just readjusting my tie and trying to keep my cowlick in place, when I heard the singing and shouting as the clock struck twelve and the band broke into "Auld Lang Syne." When I came out of the men's room, everybody had already kissed everybody else and wished them a happy New Year, and were dancing the final number.

I sat down at our empty table. We were *one*.

George finally escorted Triss back to the table, his arm possessively resting around her waist. Under his breath he said to me, "She's out of your league, Joey Boy. Better stick with Ashley." For a minute I thought of punching him in the mouth; then I reconsidered. He was at least thirty pounds bigger than me. Instead I shook hands with him, said good-night to Ashley and the rest, and drove Triss home.

"I like your friend George," she said. "Is he another one you've known all your life?"

"He's not exactly a friend," I explained. "He's just a guy I used to tag around after when I was a kid. Did he try anything with you?" I couldn't imagine that he'd done anything very serious in the middle of the dance floor, but with George, you never knew.

"Oh, he tried a few fancy new dance steps is all." She reached over and patted my hand. "Don't worry about the Georges of the world."

"How about the Joels?" I asked. "How do we stack up?"

"I'll have to think about that." I wished she were sitting closer to me, but with bucket seats and safety belts it wasn't possible. George would probably have hired a stretch limo with a driver and a back seat as big as a water bed.

"So, how long will you have to think?"

"I've already thought." In spite of the seat belt, she managed to lean over and kiss my cheek. "Ashley's really lucky, you know."

"Ashley? Why? You mean with Mel the Grinner?" Ashley was the last thing I wanted to think about just then.

"No. I mean with Joel the Jerk." I glanced over at her but she wasn't smiling, instead she was serious. "You don't even know, do you?"

I pulled into her drive, but left the motor running. It was cold outside, but I wasn't ready to let Triss go. "Know what?"

"That you and I have only this semester, less than five months. Then Ashley will have you back for the rest of her life."

I didn't like what she was saying and most of all I didn't like the matter-of-factness in her voice, which made me feel like a recycled pop can. I did the only intelligent thing I could think of—something I'd been wanting to do all evening. I unfastened my seat belt and kissed her. I kissed her until Ashley and Mel and George faded totally out of sight and until Triss acted anything but matter-of-fact.

Later, driving home alone through the empty streets, I decided that there was something to be said for New Year's Eves, after all.

When spring semester began, it wasn't at all what I had expected. I hadn't thought Ashley's being gone would make any difference, but it did. There wasn't anyone worth competing with; there was no one to trade Swifties with; there wasn't anyone to give life to the endless classes I sat through. I had thought that Triss's being there would make all the difference, but it didn't. We still didn't share any classes. My parents still kept up a quiet but persistent suggestion that I was "too young to get seriously involved." They needn't have worried, since Triss spent almost every free moment in play rehearsals. Not that I wasn't busy—tennis and golf, a ski trip over spring break, and more homework than I'd ever dreamed of. The truth is, all in all, it was a lousy semester. Fortunately, most of it happened and sort of faded away like some speeded-up film version of calendar pages being flipped by the wind.

One day, I think it was late April, I was downtown buying some tennis balls and I came out of Long's Sport Shop and this little white convertible zoomed by. I looked again, and it was Ashley. I hurried and got in my car and started tailing her. I don't think she knew I was following her, for she headed out east on the Interstate and took the fairgrounds exit. I pulled in right beside her as she parked by the horse pavilion.

"Ashley!" I called. "When'd you get this? It must pay to be a page."

Ashley slipped out from under the wheel, and I realized then it had been nearly three months since I'd seen her. She'd changed somehow. She seemed taller, but maybe it was the way she was doing her hair. It was her eyes, though, that made her look older. They had lost their shine and when she looked at me, she acted as if she were thinking of something else.

"Pays better not to be a page. I quit a couple of weeks ago."

"You're kidding! And the legislature, in gratitude, gave you the car. Right?"

"Wrong." Ashley looked at me then and grinned. It was the old Ashley back again. "It was a present from Mumsy and Dadsy. Supposedly to salve my disillusionment over the way the world is run. You know Celia and Saunders. When in doubt, buy. When Ashley's in doubt, buy twice as much. A Mercedes, no less. It is a bit much, don't you think? It's supposed to boost my ego."

I circled the convertible, inspecting its more deluxe features. "You, of course, protested."

"Certainly not. I figured I earned it. We're about as upwardly mobile as we can get. So now I'm outwardly mobile."

I leaned up against the car. "No kidding, Ashley. You couldn't have quit. And if you did, why?"

Ashley turned away and started walking toward the horse pavilion. "Why not? It seemed like a good idea at the time and it still does. If you can believe, the legislature was even worse than Bradgate High and just about as educational."

"Oh come off it, Ashley. It couldn't be that bad." I followed her. "But what are you doing out here by yourself?"

"I'm not by myself. You're here, aren't you?"

Sometimes Ashley's answers were anything but clever.

The gates to the horse pavilion were barred and padlocked. Ashley turned and headed for the horse barns. I followed her down the empty street. "I missed you, Ashley. You know why? Because you're such a pain in the lower dorsal."

She stopped and turned on me, her eyes tiny slits. "Thanks a lot!" Then she started walking again, slower. "If you really want to know, I'm trying to make up my mind about something."

I gave her a friendly pat on the shoulder. "What's the matter? You know you never have to make up your mind about anything. It's always made up— as tight as a steel trap."

"No, really," she said over her shoulder. "I'm trying to decide something."

"What's left to make up your mind about?"

The entrance to the horse barn was closed too, great wooden doors drawn across the opening.

"It's about the horse show this summer. I'm

trying to decide whether I'm going to ride or not."
She leaned up against the heavy door.

"Of course you should ride. You win again this
year and you get to keep the Logan Cup. Just think,
you can put it on your mantel to show everyone. Someday you can tell the grandchildren all
about it."

"I'm not sure it's worth the effort. Are you?"

"The competition, you mean, or the cup?"

"Either."

I couldn't understand what her problem was.

"But aren't you already entered?"

"Sure. But I can withdraw anytime, you know."
She walked slowly down the empty walk.

"Why would you want to do that? Your parents
and everybody are so proud of you when you win,
and you always do. Why break a perfect record?"
I followed a few steps behind her.

"Perfection can be boring." I could hardly make
out her words.

"Well, you could lose on purpose. That might
make it more exciting," I suggested, meaning it as
a joke. "You've done it before. Remember when
you flunked that math test on purpose?"

"I've thought of that, but it wouldn't be fair to
Life Line. Horses like to win. They really do."

"But why come out here to an empty fairground?
What's out here?"

"I don't know. I was just driving around and saw the fairgrounds exit and wondered how empty a fairgrounds would be when it was empty."

"Very empty as you can see," I said. "You could get away with murder around here and nobody'd know." I stopped in front of one of the fair's permanent buildings, a restaurant and bar with a false front that could fit into a western movie. "There's the perfect setting. Diamond Jack's." During the fair it was a busy place, but now it looked old and empty and tacky.

"Too pat. Empty fairgrounds. Empty building. No witnesses. No motive. What kind of a story could you make out of that?"

We passed a bandstand and walked down the street where the midway usually set up and crossed over to the grandstand and sat down on a park bench. For a while we just sat, neither of us talking, and as strange as it may seem I was comfortable. I knew I'd missed Ashley's jokes and laughter, but I didn't know I'd missed the closeness of her silences.

"Remember that story we read last semester where this scrivener, or whatever, was always answering, 'I prefer not to'?"

"Sure. But I never understood the story or what he was talking about."

"That's what I'm trying to decide. Do I prefer to or do I prefer not to."

I had never seen her so deadly serious. Of course I knew how important the horse show had always been to her, at least to her parents. "So have you decided?"

She stood up and brushed off her slacks. "Yes. I prefer to. But this is the last time. And then I'm going to quit forever." She leaned over, placed her hands on both my shoulders, her face inches from mine. All I could think of was that today her eyes were green.

"And do you know why, Joel? Because when I win the Logan, it will be mine to keep forever." Then she spun away with, "I'll race you to the cars."

She beat me, of course. As always, Ashley was one step beyond me. Triss was beyond me too, I was beginning to discover.

I knew that Triss wasn't exactly brilliant, but she was gorgeous, fun to be with, and she definitely made me aware that I was male. I also knew that it was a very good thing that I didn't have to worry about depending on some kind of weekly allowance from my parents. Triss's tastes were excellent and expensive, and that was just fine with me.

What wasn't so fine was her involvement in the production of *West Side Story*, which was scheduled for sometime in May. Acting, I found out, was the one thing about which Triss was totally serious, so we were a strange triangle. Ashley was committed to abstractions: world peace, ecology, human rights, animal rights. Triss was committed to but one specific: becoming a professional actress. And I was noncommittal.

That's why I couldn't understand why Triss was trying for a drama scholarship at UCLA.

"It doesn't make any sense," I told her on one of the rare nights she wasn't tied up in rehearsals. We were at Jimmy's sharing a pizza. "You don't need a scholarship. Your parents have enough money."

"That's not the point," Triss said. "A scholarship would show that I'm serious. Sort of like Marilyn Monroe's taking lessons at the Actor's Studio after she was already a star."

"But you like," I gestured around the restaurant, "all this. You don't really believe all that crap about starving artists, do you?"

"If I get a full scholarship, along with jobs in TV commercials, I won't starve." She reached across the table and took my hand. I had seen her do the same thing in rehearsals for *West Side Story*. It was effective onstage and even more so offstage, I decided. "Maybe," she continued, "there'll be another Joel."

I must have looked hurt because she patted my hand and added, "Oh, I didn't mean that quite the way it sounded. It's just that I have to prove something. I want to be first-rate. I want all the rest too: money, fame, but most of all I want to be an actress."

I didn't understand. I'd never wanted to prove anything. I didn't like being lectured to, either, even by Triss, and being serious wasn't like her. It made me uncomfortable. We never resolved the argument. We just put it on hold. That wasn't the only thing on hold. So was my time alone with Triss. It happened gradually. When evening rehearsals began, I'd pick her up afterward, we'd go out for something to eat, and I'd take her home, just the two of us.

It took about three weeks for the two of us to turn into half the cast, and it was a big cast. I'm not sure just how it happened, except that one night when Triss got into the car, she said, "I told Jill and Mario we were going for pizza and that it was okay if they came too. Okay?"

"Okay."

And it was. The three of them talked about the play and how everything was going, but then we moved on to other stuff—music and parents and even what we'd all be doing that summer. For me, music was just sound, parents something you were born with, and as to summer, I never made plans. Mom always took care of vacations. With the two of them we made four, but the next time it was three of them and Triss and me. When the group got to be ten or so, a sixth sense told me I was the odd number.

Not deliberately, but probably because they were with each other so much of the time, they began to call each other by the names they had in the play, and there were all kinds of inside jokes that I couldn't follow. When they tried—and Triss did try—to explain what was so funny, it never worked.

I finally gave up meeting her after rehearsals. Triss didn't object. Mom was ecstatic. As for Ashley, she and the Grinner were running the wheels off her Mercedes.

West Side Story was a smash. It ran three nights and a matinee. I went to the dress rehearsal and all the performances. Triss was Maria, of course. The play was sort of like *Romeo and Juliet*, and Triss made it seem so real that I felt like crying every time. Then when the play was over and Triss came out for her curtain call, the audience gave her a standing ovation every night.

Mom and Dad came with me the last night, and even they were impressed by her acting. In fact, they insisted on going backstage to tell her so.

Triss still had on her stage makeup and looked even more spectacular than usual. Dad shook her hand. Mom actually hugged her and they both gushed politely.

"For once the review in the paper was accurate," Dad said. "Marvelous production. Professional quality. And you, young lady, were perfect."

"Perfectly wonderful," Mom added. "What *are* your plans? Eventually, I mean. The stage? Movies? Television?"

"Everything!" Triss laughed, but I knew she meant it. "Television comes first though. Tomorrow, thanks to Joel." She hugged my arm and I tried to look as if I knew what she was talking about.

"Tomorrow?" Mom asked. "How? What channel? When?"

"Joel's friend George. Remember, JoJo? You introduced him at the New Year's Eve dance." I remembered, all right, but George hadn't bothered with introductions.

"He arranged a ten-minute spot on the noon show on KTTV. There'll be an interview, and I'll do a song. Isn't it fantastic?" She hugged me again. "And Joel, George'll be stopping in at the cast party. I knew you wouldn't mind. There are a couple of things we have to talk about."

"We'll be sure and watch, won't we, Joel." Mom said as she and Dad were leaving. "It's a fine opportunity and you certainly deserve it."

I walked to the parking lot with them while Triss changed. She'd said she'd meet me at my car. When my parents drove away, I sat on the fender and waited. I'd known, of course, that we'd have to go to the party, at least stop in for a little while, but my plans for the rest of the night were very specific, and they didn't include George.

It didn't take long to understand that Triss had plans of her own and they didn't include me.

I suppose it wasn't even a contest. She went to the party with me; she left the party with George. I saw her a couple of times after that before she went back to California. She didn't bother to try to explain. She didn't have to. I understood exactly why she did it.

The television interview was, as Triss would have said, "fantastic."

I suppose every life has periods of nothingness. That summer, before my senior year, started like that. Life went on even without Triss, something I once thought was impossible. The usual things happened in boring succession. School dismissed. Mom and I went up to our cottage at the lake, Dad coming up on weekends. I swam and played golf and tennis and generally lazed around with kids at the lake that I had known for years, but nothing happened, just one day following another. There should have been something I wanted to do, but I couldn't think of anything. I wasn't wasting time. I had more time than I knew what to do with until Dad cornered me one weekend.

"Can't you find something to do—something meaningful?" He sounded like old Swiftie Jacobs from Bradgate.

"Not really," I said, peering out over the lake where a Hobie Cat was trying to tack into the wind without slackening its mainsail.

"You know," he said, looking out at the sailboat as if he didn't want to look at me any more than I wanted to listen to him, "there's an old saying that goes: 'The first generation makes the money. The second spends it, and the third loses it.' You know, you've got to make something of yourself in this world and it's about time you started thinking about it."

I was tempted to ask why, but I waited for him to go on, which I knew he would do, and he did.

"Everyone has a debt to society—a debt in payment for taking up space on this planet. You should be thinking about your future and planning."

"If there is one," I muttered.

Our heart-to-heart talks usually ended the same way: Dad's giving up and going in search of Mom and my getting on my ten-speed and going off for a ride around the lake. I think he tried too hard to

be a father, applying bandages and prescribing cures
before he made a diagnosis.

Then I noticed that even Mom was getting tired
of seeing me around. I decided maybe I'd better try
to find something "meaningful" to do, and one day
I found it in a bunch of scrawny little kids known
as the Lakeside Bombers. They were a Little League
ball club, but they hadn't won a game all season.
Two coaches had given up and quit, and they were
trying to keep going on their own. I stopped by
one day to watch them practice and, incidentally,
to settle a fistfight that had erupted on the pitcher's
mound. I offered to umpire, and when it was all
over they begged me to be their coach. I'm not sure
it was what Dad had in mind as "meaningful," but
the rest of the summer, I was Joe, the Coach of the
Lakeside Bombers.

It was our last game of the season, and my Bombers had bombed out on every game and this one
looked as if it would be no different. The last inning
of the ninth, the score stood two to nothing, the
Lake Lions two and the Bombers zero, of course.
Our catcher was first up to bat, a short, fat little
kid who couldn't have more than eight inches for
a strike zone. Getting a strike across to him would
be like pitching to a potato.

"Just stand there!" I shouted in his ear. "Do you

hear me? Don't you dare take a swing at that ball!
Let them walk you!"

They did.

I looked over the rest of my Bomber crew and
picked the tiniest substitute for a pinch hitter and
told him the same thing. It worked. I think he was
too scared to swing the bat. I didn't dare try my
luck a third time, so I let Andy, our first baseman,
take his turn. There'd be no trouble finding Andy's
strike zone. He was twice as tall as the rest of the
team.

"Now listen, squirt," I said, pinioning his arms
behind his back. "If you want to amount to something in this world, you get up there and hit that
ball. He's going to throw you a strike the first pitch.
He has to. He's thrown eight straight balls already.
You swing that bat as if you're being attacked by
a real live wild lion. Get me?"

"Yes, sir," poor Andy answered, his eyes as
glassy as marbles.

I strode back to the dugout, sat down, and started
to pray to whatever fate watched over Little League
Baseball Bombers. I couldn't bear to look. The rest
of my team wasn't looking either. After all, Andy
had a batting average of something less than nothing. It was abandon-all-hope time written on every
face. I couldn't believe Ashley and I had thought,
once, that failing was a joke.

I started to gather up our gear just as I heard the crack of the bat. I looked up to see the ball arch beautifully across the bluest of blue skies and sail sweetly over the back fence. The Bombers exploded, shouting, hugging me, and giving me "low fives" and I knew then what Miss Jacobs and my dad meant by "meaningful."

"It isn't any fun to lose," I told Ashley later, after I'd filled her in on my summer at the lake.

"Maybe you have to really want something, though, to make it mean anything," she said slowly.

And I guess she was right, as usual.

One morning in late August, I drove out to the boarding stables where Ashley kept Life Line. Her white Mercedes was parked in the lot, so I parked beside it and walked over to the practice ring. It was only eight o'clock, but Ashley must have been out there since five, for she was just cooling down her horse by walking it around the ring. I stood and watched her. Even in her practice clothes, hard hat and all, Ashley looked great. The horse was a big bay—it must have stood seventeen hands—and Ashley looked so small perched in the jumping saddle. She was in complete control, of course, she and the horse moving as easily together as if they were one being. I was just about to call to her when I heard another voice from the other end of the arena.

"Great, Ashley! Just great! You do that next week, and you'll have a sure thing." The voice sounded full of white shiny teeth. I turned and walked back to my car. I'd call Ashley later.

I didn't, but I did go to the fair to see her try for the Logan Cup that she wasn't sure was worth the effort.

❈

As far as I was concerned, there were only two good spots from which to watch the horse show— standing at the rail or perched in the highest tier of seats, up next to the open windows that let in a wisp of air even on the hottest night. Mom and Dad, of course, along with Ashley's parents, and this year the Grinner, were in a kind of loge that had been occupied by my grandfather when he sponsored the first society horse show. That night I chose the rail right in front of our box, probably because it gave me a chance to turn my back on the Grinner. I don't know what there was about him that aroused my gut-felt dislike. It couldn't have been jealousy. It must have been his teeth.

I arrived late on purpose, in order to miss the first events which consisted of junior equitation, for one thing. I could think of nothing more boring than watching hordes of little kids, dressed in adult riding habits cut down to pigmy size, grimly smiling and riding around the ring on horses that cost more than our maid was paid in five years. Besides, when the kids were riding, there wasn't any space at the rail. It was filled by parents who spent the entire time waiting for their own particular kid to ride past and then leaning out and hissing, "Smile! Dammit, smile! Smile at the judge," or "Straighten up," or "Heels down! Hands in! Knees in!" It had happened to both Ashley and me. Fortunately we survived it.

By the time I propped myself against the rail, the judges' stand had been removed, the jumps had been set up, and the organ was mercifully silent. I checked out the program. There were four horses left in the competition for the Logan Cup. Three of them were from out of state—with riders whose names I'd seen on the program forever. And then there was Ashley riding Life Line.

It took three rounds to eliminate two of the horses, leaving Life Line and a huge Hanoverian named Show Boat to compete in a timed jump-off. It took a while to raise the jumps and change the course, and I considered going back to where Ashley and Life Line were waiting, but the Grinner had already headed in that direction. Besides, Ashley would not be in a talking mood; she'd be a knot of solid concentration, planning exactly how she would approach each jump. If the Grinner thought she'd be ready for chitchat, he was going to be surprised.

The next round was a stalemate. Both horses committed one fault and their times were identical. Jumps were reset and raised and it began to look as if the event could go on all evening. Show Boat made a clean round, but a near refusal at the double oxers slowed his time. Then it was Ashley and Life Line.

I marveled once again at how someone as small as she could control, could dominate the big bay gelding. Perched on the jumping saddle she should have looked ridiculous, but somehow, despite the severity of the hunt clothes she wore, Ashley was almost beautiful.

When she took the first jump, I held my breath. They cleared it with a foot to spare and came out of it in perfect position for the next, but I wanted to shout at her to slow down. She was pushing Life Line to his limit and each time they approached a jump, the audience grew silent, then let out a collective gasp as she cleared it. Life Line rushed the final jump, a wall that had been raised another six inches, and I closed my eyes so that I couldn't see what I was sure would happen. Ashley had lost a stirrup on the previous jump, and I imagined Life Line crashing into the wall, then a tangle of reins and thrashing hooves and Ashley caught beneath.

The crowd exploded into applause and cheers and I opened my eyes to see Ashley calmly circling the ring. When she rode past me, she slowed enough to give me a grin of pure triumph and leaning toward me said, "Come help me untack—I've done enough work for one night." Then she was gone.

The ride for the Logan Cup had been the last event of the show, so the horse barns were pretty nearly empty by the time I got there. The boarding stable where Life Line stayed would haul him back; the big six-horse trailer was already pulled up near the entrance. Even though most of the horses were gone, the place still smelled of them and hay and sweet feed.

Ashley already had the saddle off and was standing, reins hooked over her arm, talking to the rider she had bested in the jump-off. He was twice as big as Ashley and three times as old, but when he bent toward her, I didn't think he remembered the difference in their ages.

I waited till he left, then helped Ashley switch from bridle to halter and held on to Life Line while she groomed him. He was so big and she was so small that she had to stand on a stool to reach his withers.

"Where's the Grin . . . where's old Mel?" I asked, expecting to see his teeth glowing in the semi-darkness.

"I sent him home with my parents and the Cup," she said, undoing and brushing out the braids in the gelding's mane. "It was a good ride, but I couldn't stand one more instant replay. When something's over, why talk about it?"

It occurred to me that maybe whatever she'd had with Mel was also over. "So what am I doing here? Besides holding on to your horse? How do you know I don't want to discuss your equestrian feats, jump by jump?"

She finished with the horse and gave him a swat on the rump. "Because, Joel Logan the Third, you are utterly, completely, absolutely predictable and you've never made the mistake of paying me a compliment in your life. You are here because you are going to take me for a ride on the Ferris wheel, and then, like the gentleman you are supposed to grow into, you're going to escort me safely to my car."

"Ferris wheel?" My stomach tightened.

The kid from the boarding stable loaded Life Line into the van while I stood staring at Ashley. "Did you say Ferris wheel? You mean that machine with the lights that goes in circles and pumps money out of stupid thrillseekers?"

Ashley nodded.

Although Ashley knew almost everything about me and could usually guess the rest, motion sickness was not one of those things. When I was a little kid, one circle on the playground merry-go-round was enough to start my stomach doing push-ups. I was okay on planes, even on boats if they kept moving, but circles—even the very word made my teeth ache.

"You can't mean that glittering monster that's loaded with half the population of the state, all of whom will be spilling popcorn and probably barfing because of the dizzying heights?"

Ashley nodded and smiled.

"Why don't we just do the midway? Or how about the Old Mill? We haven't been in that since we were kids."

"I want," Ashley said, with exaggerated diction and dignity, "to experience the sensation of going in a circle that *I* have chosen. Besides, it'll be good practice. Getting there, I mean. Come on."

"Getting there? I don't understand."

"I'll tell you later."

I looked down at her for a minute as she stood there, her chin thrust out in sheer stubbornness, her hair ruffled from the hard hat she'd discarded, her shiny riding boots, her shirt of pure silk, and the eighteen-carat pin in her stock. I shrugged and followed her. I couldn't let her go by herself. Someone would be sure to rip her off.

The smell was unbelievable—stale grease, cheap perfume, and sweating bodies. The noise was worse. My stomach was doing somersaults already just at the thought of the Ferris wheel. I gave it one last try. "Do you think they'll take a credit card? I may not have enough cash."

She let go of my arm and tickled me in the ribs. "Keep walking. I'm treating."

We soon learned that you didn't just *get* on a Ferris wheel; you *wait* on a Ferris wheel along with a frantic mother and her four untamed offspring, a gaggle of giggling girls who kept eyeing Ashley's outfit and whispering to each other, and several half-grown guys in blue jeans clinging like skin to their legs and each wolfing down a hamburger and talking at the same time.

Ashley stared straight ahead at the garish lights that outlined the giant wheel against the darkness of the sky. She was pretending she was invisible, I could tell, and it wasn't until we were locked in our chair by a tired-looking operator that she turned to me and said, "Quit looking so grim. This is supposed to be fun. This is what real people do."

Our seat jerked forward and upward and we sat suspended just above the heads of midway walkers. "It's fun. It's fun," I agreed through gritted teeth. "How long do you suppose the ride lasts?"

"Don't talk about endings, Joel. We haven't even begun." She sat, elbows on the safety bar, looking out across the midway.

Just at the moment when I thought I was going to lose it all on some innocent bystander, the machine jerked, the music came on, and we were lofted into the coolness of the evening air, not one minute too soon.

As we reached the top, Ashley leaned over and patted my hand. "Are you okay?"

I thought I'd heard every sound her voice could make, but this was new. It was concern, not teasing. "Sure. I'm great. Why?"

"Because you look peculiar in that particular shade of green. Besides, it doesn't match your shirt." It was the old Ashley.

I thought about sticking out my tongue and changed my mind. I knew what she meant about green. Then I remembered that I didn't know about something else she'd said earlier. "What did you mean about practicing? You said that getting to the Ferris wheel would be good practice. Practice for what? You planning on joining the girlie show?" I gestured to the tent beneath us where a sad-looking woman in a beaded dress was sort of jiggling to the beat of a tired drum.

"I'll tell you later. Right now let's forget who we are. We're just two kids from some little town, and this is the single most exciting time of our lives, and our parents are over there in the grandstand listening to country western music. We've known each other forever, of course, so they trust us implicitly." She frowned. "They trust *me*. You have been known to drag Main in your family pickup on Saturday nights when you were supposed to be at choir practice. How does that sound?"

"If my stomach hadn't already turned, I'd tell you. Why choir practice?"

"Because that's what real people do. Besides, what else is there to do in a small town?"

"What do you know about small towns?" I asked.

"I read."

"What's so unreal about us? Just the way we are?" We dropped down and before I could gasp, we were jerked up again and for a scant breath we were above everything and the world around us was nothing but a glare of lights and a blare of music.

I thought I heard her say, amid the screams from the giggling gaggle in the seat ahead of ours, "Everything!" Then we swooped around again and when we reached the top of the arc, the Ferris wheel stopped and we swung, weightless and waiting.

"Wonder how long we're going to be up here," I said, hoping I could keep my stomach on hold.

"Five dollars' worth," Ashley answered. "Hope nobody is waiting for anybody. I paid the man five dollars to stop us at the top. A dollar a minute isn't bad, is it? You'd use up that much scooping the loop twice in your pickup."

I gave up and relaxed.

"I just managed the impossible. I stopped time. See, we can almost hold it," she said, motioning at the fairgrounds beneath and the city which spread beyond.

Dad always said a man couldn't buy time with money. He was wrong. Ashley had done just that. Maybe it was the intensity of her voice or maybe it was because I no longer felt as if I were going one way and the rest of the universe another, but the view at which she was pointing *did* hold a small magic in its glow. "So what should we do with all this time we have—besides hold it?" I wasn't trying to tease her. I was serious.

Ashley relaxed and leaned back in the seat, making it sway slowly. "Share the world with each other. See things from a new perspective."

"That last jump must have scrambled your brain. You don't sound like you." She didn't. She sounded far away, even though she was sitting next to me. There was a kind of seriousness in her voice that I hadn't heard before.

"That's the problem, Joel. I'm finding out I don't know who me is, or maybe I'm discovering that I don't like the me I do know. It's hard to explain."

"That's crazy. You're Ashley. Top of the TAGS. Winner of the Logan Cup, and probably Bradgate High's next valedictorian if we can make it through another school year." It was all true, of course, but I thought I could make her laugh at it as she always did. I was wrong.

"None of that matters. None of it's really important. Don't you see? I've spent all my life doing things that don't take any effort and that don't make any real difference in the world. I might as well have never existed."

It all sounded stupid to me and I told her so, ending up with, "You're just suffering from post-equine depression. What you really need is to beat me at tennis. How about tomorrow at ten?" Our five minutes and Ashley's five dollars must have run out because the Ferris wheel started moving again and lowered us toward the ground.

"Maybe you're right," she said, but she didn't sound convinced. "Or maybe it's just because summer is almost over and we have to start the whole routine again. Circles on a Ferris wheel are infinitely preferable."

"So what about tennis?" I asked as we jerked to a stop and were released from our cage.

"Can't," Ashley said as we threaded our way back toward the horse pavilion. "Mother and Father are hauling me into Chicago for C and C."

"What's that?" As we neared the parking lot, the noise and the people disappeared.

"Culture and clothes. Or maybe it's the other way around. We'll be back sometime next week. Call me and I'll beat you then."

I waited until she unlocked her car door and was inside with the motor running. "Great. Want me to follow you home?"

"You've got to be kidding." She smiled up at me. "You couldn't keep up. And besides, I'm not going to self-destruct and ruin a perfectly good car." She patted the car door and took off with a low whine of her tires. I watched her turn out of the gate and decided I'd seen enough of the fair, too.

School began again with three pointless, futile days before the Labor Day weekend, just enough time for kids to show off suntans and new clothes, enough time for us to walk through our classes as if we and the teachers had to practice for the year that was about to happen.

The first morning, Ashley and I arrived at the school parking lot at almost the same time, five minutes late, as usual, and she got the last vacant spot, so I had to park semi-illegally on the grass. For once, she waited for me, so I didn't have to lope to catch up with her and, instead of her usual intensity, she was smiling a self-satisfied pixie grin.

"What's with you? Did you talk the school into letting you graduate without going through senior year?"

"Hadn't thought of that. . . ." She let her voice trail away as if we were in the middle of a conversation we'd begun hours earlier. "Do you suppose they'd consider it? If I promise to come to homeroom every day?"

"They've already considered something. Otherwise you wouldn't be looking so happy. Or is it because we're finally seniors?" I slowed my steps to match hers, which were about as slow as she could possibly walk. "Besides, what's so bad about school? It's better than doing nothing."

"Mr. Perfect." She stopped just outside the front doors. "For someone who's both talented and gifted, you can be . . . you can be very dense. Don't you remember from philosophy class that there are never only two alternatives? In this case there are three: school, work, or nothing. Nothing sounds boring. Besides, I think there's a law against nothing if you're under eighteen."

We made it through the front door and then into the main hall. The smell was kind of welcoming in a school sort of way—cleaning compound, disinfectant, chalk dust, and paper. At least, after eleven years it smelled familiar. I glanced at the hall clock. We were ten minutes late, which really didn't matter because on the first day homeroom lasted forever, as if we were all in some kind of conspiracy to hold on to summer vacation as long as possible.

"But why so happy on the first day of school?"

We'd finally reached the door to our homeroom, which, of course, was empty. I'd forgotten about the assembly. I had a feeling Ashley hadn't. I headed toward the auditorium, Ashley at my elbow. When we topped the stairs, Ashley tugged me down until we were sitting together on the top step.

"You won't believe it," she said, locking her hands and leaning back against the bannister. "Only mornings."

"Only mornings what?"

She yawned much too elaborately. "Just mornings: homeroom, French 4, physics, advanced calculus. Then nothing but freedom and responsibility."

"What's that? Freedom and responsibility. A new course?"

"Not really. I'm only going to go to school in the morning. In the afternoon I work on my independent study. Don't you like the sound of it? Independent study."

"What are you going to study? The life cycle of the moss plant?" I always had trouble trying to be sarcastic with Ashley. Not that she didn't get it, but she pretended she didn't and insisted on taking it literally. I should have learned that was her way of beating me at my sarcasm game.

"Oh, no. That has been done, and very conclusively, years ago by Comstock, if I remember." She sounded so sincere I almost believed her.

"I give up," I said. "What's the big project that's going to take all your afternoons for a semester?"

"Not just the semester. For the whole year. I'm going to be tutoring in the Alternative School."

"You mean down on Third Street? Working with a bunch of dropouts?"

"That's the point. They're not dropping out. They're dropping in." Her face beamed like a TV evangelist's.

"You've lost your mind! Here I thought you were going to dedicate your life to abolishing compulsory education and Bradgate High in particular, and now you tell me you're going to be going to school double time." There were moments when I was with Ashley that I could badger her with what I thought was my superior logic—lead her on so she would fix me with a vacant stare, her teeth clenched, and without another word walk away pretending I didn't exist. This time, she didn't.

"You're just jealous. Besides you're being pro-

vincial, parochial, and, what's worse, the equivalent
of a party pooper. Plus which you have all the
compassion of a squid." She managed to sound
maddeningly superior.

"Why a squid?" I asked. "What do you have
against squids?"

"Nothing, but they are basically not too bright.
In fact, their IQ probably matches yours. And when
they get confused, they throw out clouds of ink,
which is what you do all the time, only with
words." She looked at me triumphantly.

A bell rang, announcing the end of the assembly,
and we barely missed being stampeded as teachers
and pupils erupted from the double doors, but
worst of all I missed my chance to get back at
Ashley. But I could never get even with her. We
were always at opposite ends of a teeter-totter,
looking either down or up but never quite leveling
with each other.

I did manage to get in one final, "Why, Mother
Theresa, do you harbor this innate urge to guide
the blind and reform the world?" as we were pushed
down the hall by the thundering horde of fellow
students.

Ashley stopped, turned to me, and in her familiar
fierce voice said, "You don't need a reason *for* doing
something. You need a reason for *not* doing it."

That was the closest Ashley had ever come to explaining how her head worked, and though I listened, I still didn't understand.

It was the usual first homeroom that morning with Mr. Bowman passing out the Bradgate High School calendars. They weren't just computerized lists; they were first-class, A number one, four-color jobs, pictures of this year's seniors on every page, and the inevitable boxes for each day of the month, most of them filled with school activities, even the weekends. Just looking at it made me feel as if I were wearing a necktie, or maybe a noose.

I turned to see Ashley's reaction. We were given these calendars every year, of course, and, each time, she'd managed a new and varied look of sheer agony. This time she was smiling, sitting there and actually smiling at the stupid calendar, and when she saw me watching her, she winked. Ashley never wasted winks. They always meant that she'd just come up with some kind of off-the-wall idea.

"Look at January," she said quietly.

I dutifully flipped the pages to the right month. The picture was a composite made up of photographs that must have been taken when we were in the first grade. I recognized a lot of the kids: David, Kristin, Michael, Meridith, Rob, and Emily. I was there, too, scowling directly at the camera, but Ashley, who should have been standing next to me, was missing. The space was there, of course, where she'd been, but where a six-year-old should have been there was only a white blank.

"Weird," I said as Bowman went through the yearly ritual of assigning lockers. "How did you manage that?"

"Liquid Paper. That stuff you use to cover up typing mistakes. It works on negatives too." She turned around in her seat and spoke to me directly. "I corrected an error."

"What error?"

"Native Americans believe that if your image is captured by a camera, your soul is captive too. I set myself free."

"What about your senior picture? For the yearbook? They won't let you out of high school unless you have a picture to prove you've survived thirteen years of American education."

"I can always have my picture taken with my back to the camera."

"So you can't face it?" I was baiting her, I knew, but Ashley could never resist an argument.

"I can face it. I just can't stomach it. It's a rite of passage that I'm going to pass up." She flipped through the calendar. "And here's another thing that's positively, perfectly pass-up-able."

I looked at the box she was pointing at—the senior prom in May, just a couple of weeks before graduation. "Oh no you don't!" I said. "You promised you'd go with me. I'm already saving my allowance for your corsage."

For probably the first time in our lives, I'd managed to surprise Ashley, and for one of the first times, at least for a few seconds, she was speechless, looking at me as if I'd lost my mind.

"Junior-high dance. Remember? Carla Wilson wouldn't go with me. She called me a nerd, and when you and I walked home together you promised we'd go to the senior prom together because probably no one else would want to go with us."

"You still are. A nerd, I mean. Did I promise?"

"Well, you didn't cross your heart or sign an affidavit or anything, but you sounded pretty definite at the time."

"Okay," she said with an exaggerated sigh, "but I'll bet I said I'd go *to* the dance with you. That doesn't mean we actually have to go inside."

A bell signalled the end of homeroom, and we launched ourselves into the last year of high school. That semester Ashley worried about the future. I let things happen. Ashley thought she had to change the world. I went along for the ride. Ashley believed without hope. I hoped without belief.

"Do you realize the polar ice cap is melting? In another thousand years . . ."

"Really?"

"We're polluting our environment. Someday..."

"So?"

"How do you know but what the nuclear bomb won't go off any minute?"

"I don't."

"But think! One push of a button and our entire future will be wiped out."

"Maybe."

"But can't you see? We may be preparing ourselves for a world that will never exist."

Ashley could not compromise. She was a persistent perfectionist in an imperfect world.

"Maybe I should join the Peace Corps."

"They won't take you. You're too young."

"I could be a one-person, teenage peace mission to Russia."

"It's been done. Remember Samantha?"

❧

I think, that semester, I was her touchstone to test the practicality of her lofty projects or maybe I was the only person who always said no to her yes.

We didn't have any classes together, and it was strange because ever since grade school we had always been together. I caught up to her in the hall one noon after school had been going on for a couple of weeks. "How are you and your dropouts coming? Have you talked them into reenlisting in the school system?"

She was hurrying down the hall on her way to the parking lot, and she kept on hurrying, not necessarily trying to ignore me but more as if she had something far more important to take up her time.

"Don't be an intellectual snob. Dropouts have reasons for dropping out. I'm trying to give them reasons for dropping in."

I hurried ahead and held the door open as she dashed through. "It's wonderful what you're doing, Ashley—saving the illiterates of the world." I couldn't believe that Ashley, who was always late for homeroom, was actually rushing to get to a different school in the afternoon.

She stopped suddenly and turned on me, her eyes colorless. "Poor old sarcastic Joel. You really don't understand do you? That there's a whole other world out there that's lots more important than Bradgate High and playing racquetball or going swimming at the club."

She turned then and left me standing, still holding the door open. It slowly occurred to me that she really was serious, that what she was doing meant more to her than escaping the endless afternoons at Bradgate. As for me, the whole thing seemed depressing and boring. I finally closed the door, shrugged, and went off to my art class.

A few weeks later, having caught only glimpses of Ashley dashing from a classroom or hurrying down the hall or waving to me as she pulled out of the parking lot, I decided just for the hell of it to drop in on Ashley and her dropouts.

Classes had been cancelled that afternoon for some kind of teachers' meeting, so I drove over to the Alternative School. The name intrigued me— Alternative School. I wasn't sure whether it suggested freedom of choice or if it was a threat: "This place or you've had it, Buster!"

Ashley's car wasn't in the parking lot, but I went into the building anyway and hunted up the school secretary, who frowned at me at first as if I were an intruder, but then relented when she found out I was looking for Ashley.

"Her class is just about over, but you can wait for her. I'll show you where she is." As we climbed the stairs in what once must have been a junior high school, she added, "That girl is something else, isn't she? When she first came, no one thought she'd last through the first afternoon. Were we wrong! She's the best thing that's happened around here since they put in the sandwich machine."

As I stood in the hall, I couldn't quite figure out

if the comparison was a compliment or a put-down. The door was open and I could see Ashley, perched on the edge of a desk, explaining in a patient monotone the sound of vowels in words ending with *e*.

"The first vowel says its own name, *if*," she said, pointing to the blackboard, "the word ends with an '*e*.' *B-i-d-e*, bide. *B-i-d*, bid. See, the *i* says its name, but take the *e* off and it becomes a short sound: bid. Same with hide, hid. Ride, rid." Her students, five in all, surrounded her, sprawled in arm-desk chairs, one girl studying Ashley's Bass Weejuns, another filing her nails, a boy staring out the window, and two others staring at Ashley.

"Now, Brenda," Ashley went on, "what are these two words?" She pointed to "fade" and "fad."

Brenda looked up from her nails. "What was that again? I guess I was thinking of something else."

"Perhaps," Ashley went on, sounding every bit like Mrs. Kennedy, our first-grade teacher of long ago, "Sonya can help you."

Smiling, Sonya looked up from Ashley's shoes as if awakened from a pleasant dream. "Base? Bass?"

The boys laughed, Brenda stopped filing her nails, Sonya blushed, and Ashley giggled. "Wrong words; interesting idea. Maybe we should concentrate on learning to read from looking at labels."

Then everyone began to talk at once. I left; I couldn't bear to watch. Ashley, one of the most brilliant students at Bradgate, wasting her time with a bunch of losers. Then I remembered my Lakeside Bombers, who had turned into winners. But that was different. I was just killing time. Ashley was killing herself.

I tried to call her two or three times on weekends after that, but she was never home until one Saturday late in October.

"Where have you been?" I asked, realizing it was a question that I'd never bothered to ask her before. "I never get a chance to talk to you in homeroom and you must disappear on weekends."

"Here and there. In and out. Up and down. Around and back. Down and out." She sounded as if she were grinning. "I'll tell you where I haven't been. Dullsville."

"I think you've gone somewhere else." I held the phone at arm's length and yelled into it, "BON-KERS! You've gone BONKERS!"

She wasn't just grinning, she was laughing. "You sound like the spoiled little boy I used to know. So what have you been doing?"

"The usual," I said, wishing I could think of something more exciting. "How about tennis? You owe me a game from last summer."

"I'm sorry, Joel." I didn't think she sounded particularly sad. "I'm going on a retreat with the kids. It's an overnight at the Y camp."

I almost dropped the phone. "Retreat with the kids? I thought retreats were for monks or nuns or something. And what kids?"

Her voice was as patient as it had been the afternoon I'd listened to her in the classroom. "Some of the teachers and some of the students at the Alternative School are spending the afternoon and night out in the country in order to interact in a different setting."

I must have sounded less than enthusiastic, because before she hung up she said, "Look, I really have to go now. They'll be waiting for me. But how about picking me up at school some afternoon next week? I'll tell you all about it then. Or if you can't make it next week, the week after. Okay?"

It wasn't exactly okay, though I wasn't sure why. Anyway, I figured I'd see her on Monday or Tuesday afternoon; but then I had a bunch of stuff to do after school and it wasn't until over a week later that I parked in front of the Alternative School to wait for Ashley.

I sat there for almost an hour and I was just getting ready to leave, when Ashley appeared. Walking out with her were the window-staring boy and the fingernail girl, Brenda, who looked a lot different standing up than she did sitting down. In fact, she looked as if she should be headed for the maternity ward.

They all stood talking and laughing until Ashley finally spotted me, broke away, and got into the car. She was still smiling.

"I suppose you're going to be the fairy god-mother?" I said. "But why's she bothering to learn to read? It's a little late now, isn't it?" I didn't really mean it, but I was ticked off at having waited so long.

Ashley shook her head. "The only problem Brenda had with reading was that she couldn't see any reason to try. She has a reason now. Obviously. And she is learning. And Joel, do me a favor. Don't try to be blasé and sophisticated. Just be your natural, moronic self."

"Okay, okay," I said starting the car. "It's your life. Where's the Mercedes?"

"It's home where it lives in the afternoons. It didn't take me long to learn to use the bus."

"Why? Afraid they'd steal the hubcaps?"

"Somebody might," she admitted, "but not these kids. Not anymore. It just wasn't right, like show-ing off. Anyway, I like the bus. There's always somebody to talk to and it makes the ride seem shorter. But that's not the important part."

We were back on the freeway, heading across town, but the echo of triumph in Ashley's voice made me pull into the slow lane and ease my foot off the gas. I knew she had a secret and she knew I knew it. She also knew that I wouldn't be able to resist asking. I tried to sound disinterested. "So what's important enough to make you look happy?"

She turned toward me, her eyes bright blue, her smile contagious. No wonder Bradgate had seemed so dull without her around. "There's going to be an article in the paper. About the kids I've been tutoring. All of them will be back in regular school next semester. Except Brenda, and she'll be back, too, as soon as she can after the baby's born. Their pictures will be there and everything. Isn't that great?"

"What's so great about that?" I asked.

"Joel, don't you see? There's nothing wrong with these kids except they've always felt like losers, second rate. This article will be all about how great they really are, about how hard they're trying. About how they're going to make it." I wanted to tell her that the last time she'd sounded that enthusiastic was when she'd played Lennon and Mc-Cartney's "Yesterday" for me for the first time.

I pulled in the drive in front of her house and turned off the ignition. "So when is all this going to happen? Do you want me to get extra copies of the paper? No kidding. I will if you want me to.

And actually, it is terrific. You've really pulled it off."

"It'll be in tomorrow's paper. See, Joel, it doesn't have anything to do with me. It's the kids and the chance and the teachers. And it worked—at least for these five kids it's working. The secret is to make them want to learn. They'd sort of run out of steam and decided it's all hopeless. And they have so little self-esteem. . . ." She reached over and gave me a one-arm hug. It felt so good I wondered how a two-arm hug would feel.

"Okay." I said. "Since everything is so wonderful, how about a celebration? But only if you promise not to talk about drop-ins and dropouts."

"What kind of celebration? When? Where? My answer is yes, but tell me."

I'd thought of it just two minutes earlier, but I hoped it sounded like a good idea. "Somebody gave Dad a couple of tickets to the Minnesota game this weekend. Why don't we drive up on Saturday, take a look at the campus, go to the game: popcorn, hot dogs, and all. How about it?"

She looked surprised. "When did you become a football fan?"

"About the same time those kids became winners."

She got out of the car.

"What about Minneapolis?" I asked again. "Want

to go? The world can do without us for one day."

"Just *one* day?" She started to close the door. "I'll let you know. By Friday. But first I'll have to learn the rules of the game, won't I?"

"It might help."

I tried to catch Ashley the next day in school, but I couldn't find her. The more I thought about my idea of our going up to the football game, the more I thought how much fun it would be to take Ashley. I don't know whether I was finally growing up or whether I was realizing something I'd never really thought of before. I had always taken Ashley for granted, but she deserved more than that. I wondered if she'd always known what I was just discovering.

After my last morning class, I hied myself out to the parking lot only to see Ashley wheeling out of the drive.

"Hey, Ashley!" I shouted, sprinting after the Mercedes.

She turned, waved, smiled, and sped down the street.

After school, I drove downtown and picked up five copies of the afternoon paper. I sprawled out on the den couch and opened the paper to the feature page. There was a three-column spread of Ashley's home, and smiling out at me from an inset in the upper right-hand corner was Ashley. The banner across the top of the page read, "Well-Known Brad-gate High Senior Devotes Free Time to Helping Dropouts." There were no pictures of Ashley's five. Instead, at the bottom on the page was a collage of pictures that some enterprising reporter had dug out of the newspaper morgue: Ashley in front of the bear's cage, Ashley winning the club's junior tennis tournament, Ashley being chosen the representative Bradgate TAG, Ashley winning the Logan Cup. I skimmed through the article. A couple of the teachers were named, but there was no mention of a Brenda or a Sonya or the sad-eyed boy who stared out the window.

Ashley would be crushed. Furious. She'd just die. Knowing Ashley, I was positive she'd never go back to the Alternative School. She would have lost their trust. She could never face them. I tried to call her—she had her own phone—but there was no answer. I tried again. I tried after dinner and she still didn't answer, so I gave up and settled down to hit the books, for I had a tough test coming up the next day. About eleven o'clock I tried once more, still with no luck, so I went to bed.

Hours later, it felt like, I awoke with a start. Mom was standing at the foot of my bed. "Do you have any idea where Ashley is? Her mother is on the phone. She's not home."

"She's not home?" I repeated, trying to make some sense of what I thought was a bad dream.

"Did you see her today?"

All I could make out in the darkness was my mother, silhouetted against the hall light.

"Sure. In school."

"After school, Joel?"

It wasn't a bad dream. I was awake now. "I saw her leave. In her car. I waved. She waved back. That was at noon. Why? What's wrong?"

"She hasn't come home, and it's almost two. They're going to notify the police. You'd better get dressed, Joel."

"Should I go out and look for her?" I asked, still half dazed as I reached for my clothes.

"I don't think so. She may have had an accident. Your father's calling the hospitals now. Joel, does she drive by herself down to that school?"

"She takes a bus and walks the rest of the way. Why?"

"Well, you know that neighborhood. I never did think it was safe for her. Did she say anything to you about any plans? Celia says her car is gone."

I pulled on a T-shirt and followed Mom downstairs. "Her car! I didn't get to talk to her this noon. I just yelled at her. She waved and drove off."

Dad, still in his pajamas, came in from the den. "No accidents reported. That's one good thing.

Joel, do you know any reason why she'd go off by herself like this without telling anyone?"

"You know Ashley," I said, trying not to show how mad I was getting at Ashley's stupidity. "She never needs a reason for doing anything. She only needs a reason for not doing something."

"We'd better go over, don't you think?" Mom started back up the stairs. "Saunders and Celia asked if we could. Maybe she ran away. Celia said she threatened to once when . . ."

"That was in the eighth grade," I said. "And she wasn't running away. She just wanted to join a Greenpeace expedition."

Later, in the car, Dad half turned toward me as I sat hunched in the back seat. "Don't misunderstand me, Joel, but is Ashley involved . . . with . . . drugs and alcohol?"

"You mean is she doing drugs? No! And she doesn't drink and she's not pregnant, either. In fact," I said in a burst of complete illogic, "we have a first date this weekend."

Saunders and Celia met us at the door, both completely dressed as if they had just come in from an evening out. Mom hugged Celia, and Saunders put his arm around Dad's shoulder and led him into the rec room. "I think we'd all better have a drink," Saunders said, as Mom and Celia sat down on the couch. At first I thought it was anger that started to crawl up my throat—anger that they were acting so normal, so constrained, and then I knew it wasn't anger. It was fear. Ashley didn't do stupid things like this. Someone had kidnapped her. Or if not, someone had stolen her car and dumped her off to find her way home.

We must have sat there for hours. The police came, listened, took a couple of Ashley's pictures and left. They'd keep a lookout, they said, keep checking the hospitals, and they'd send out the car license and description over their shortwave. They asked questions about the same things my father had suggested: Drugs? Alcohol? Boyfriend? Family squabble? There were many questions, but no answers.

"And you saw her this noon?" The officer turned toward me. "How did she look?"

I thought about it a long time, remembering the wave of her arm, the flash of her smile. "She looked," I finally said, "she looked happy."

Mom convinced Celia to lie down on the couch and try to sleep and Saunders agreed there was nothing further any of us could do but wait, so we left with their promise that they would call us the minute they heard anything.

We were home only about half an hour when the phone rang. Mom answered.

"Oh, that's wonderful! Where?"

That dumb Ashley! I looked at my watch. It was

five-thirty in the morning and I had a test in three more hours.

"Is she all right?"

There was a pause that grew into a long silence punctuated with Mom's "Oh! Oh no! We'll be right over."

"Where is she?" I was shouting.

Mom turned from the phone, her voice as pale as her face. "Out at the fairgrounds. In the parking lot near the horse pavilion."

I already felt the answer, but I asked anyway, "Is she all right?"

"Joel," she began and reached out for my father. "She's dead."

"Who?" I screamed. All I could think of was one of the kids in the Alternative School.

"They found an empty pill bottle on the seat of her car. She must have taken them all."

"She couldn't! She wouldn't!" I was shouting again. "Not Ashley!"

Time does not stand still. It always keeps moving just as it did after that night. It moved through days of classes that I didn't attend. It moved through newspaper articles and television news. It moved through the funeral and through the rest of that long, long senior year. It moved and I moved with it, but I didn't live it.

For the first few weeks, all I could think of was Ashley—and her "kaleidoscope" eyes. One day I went up to my room, took out all the Beatles records Ashley had given me for my various birthdays, sat on the edge of my bed, and broke every single one. After that my anger at her closed out almost everything.

At home I felt as if I were under a parental microscope, my every word assessed, my every move checked as if I might decide to follow Ashley's stupid example. They needn't have bothered. I spent my days grinning when I felt like screaming, smiling when I felt like crying, and partying so I wouldn't have to be alone.

But in spite of all that, I lived that awful moment of the telephone call over and over, trying to piece the fragments of the real Ashley together, caught in a nightmare of "whys" that no one could answer. How many hours in a semester? How many hours can a person cry? Not with tears, but inside where the salt burns.

I didn't go to the senior prom. I didn't even go to graduation. It was the summer before my first year of college and my parents were planning to leave for the lake. They wanted me to go with them. I didn't.

Instead, I went to the fair.

PART IV

✖

Joel

Sounds faded to an eerie, restless quiet as the fair-grounds emptied in the early-morning hours. Joel still sat alone in the horse pavilion, staring down at the darkened show ring.

Hadn't Ashley known that death was final? The End. Period. Why? Why did she do it? It couldn't have been just the article. She must have thought of doing it before. Was it because of something he had done? Something he didn't do? Why hadn't she told him if she was hurting that much?

She'd said that when one link dropped out of the chain of life, something was lost and could never be replaced. But that was only a lousy frog!

Then, as if Ashley were there to hear him, the thoughts became words, shouted. "Ashley! You didn't have to do it! And you didn't do it just to yourself! You killed a part of *me*. It was selfish! Ashley, it was dumb! Why couldn't you wait for tomorrow?" The sound echoed back from the rafters.

A sliver of dawn crept through the dome windows and the harsh cawing of crows began another day. Joel stood and walked stiffly down the steep wooden steps. The rest of the fair was still asleep except for a solitary police car cruising the empty street.

Joel hesitated in the doorway. To the left stood the livestock barns where Ben, Naomi, and Stella would soon be waking for their two-hour ride home. To the right, up the hill past the midway, Kentucky Rose might be dreaming of Nashville nights.

And Ashley? Under the brightening sky, Joel knew that Ashley was gone forever, knew that as long as he lived he might never understand Ashley's *why not*. But maybe, just maybe, if Ben or Kentucky Rose or somebody would listen, he could try to explain what the matter was, try to sort out the broken pieces of the past and begin living a life without Ashley.

Joel took a deep breath of the morning freshness and stepped out from the shadow of the horse pavilion. It was time to go home from the fair.